Chapter 1

There came a day when I realized I never got to where I was on my own. I had help. And, without doubt, if it hadn't been for that assistance, my story could not be told. I existed because of *Mead*, a vast system that controlled humanity — This purveyor of souls was created by *God*.

Mead collected data on individuals — The information went up the chain to *Higher Authorities. It* taught lessons to each human born into this World. *It* managed mankind for *God* and *His Executives*: *Jesus*, *Mohammed* and *Buddha*, who oversaw their religious masses, with one exception, Judaism. The Jews had no *Executive*, they went straight to the top.

My Life, under *Mead's* auspices was a magic gone amuck. *It* existed from the moment of my conception, another event, which was, also, carefully planned and controlled, through my entire existence, until the day, when I reached my expiration date.

Mead managed many worlds within our world. I lived in the largest sector; the good-bad world; it had its ups and downs. There was, also, the really-good world, which was allocated to the very few. This world was never to be confused with the material world because that was reserved, mostly, for gluttons; people who worshiped money. The worst, by far, were those from the bad-evil world, or the just plain evil. It too was for the very few. It had great strength; however, and impacted all of the other worlds. Its power has always dominated human history.

Even so, somehow goodness never died; it persevered. People on the good-side built the world. People on the bad-side destroyed it. All the while, the vast majority of the people sat back and did absolutely nothing. Things happened regardless.

Conflict was a tool, of *Mead's*, to manage goodness. Really-good humans, however, never sought conflict; but the maker of mischief, mania, magic, and mayhem made sure that they always got their fair share. They were, also, prone to tragedy because they were never protected by the *m-workers*; *Mead's* muscle.

As for me, I should've been incarcerated early in life but because *Mead* called the shots, I never had a say in the matter. I clearly recalled matters that stemmed back to when I was a mere ten years old. I had no control over what I did. *Mead* was my choreographer. I was *its* dancer. When I planned to do something, especially if my intentions were good, I failed because I had no goodness in me. Any effort fell dead before it breathed life because, without fanfare, *Mead* thwarted it. On the other hand if I planned and carried out something nefarious; *it* opened every door for me.

Mead intervened in my affairs time and again. But, I never had an awareness because I was blinded by its power. I went through my early years oblivious to anything good; life was always what I wanted at any particular moment; nefarious or not.

Mead had complete control, as if I was his hacked computer, and that I moved at *its* every whim. As an adult I would be punished by daily torture sessions; morning, noon and night – My life unfolded unconventionally. During my early years, I had no goals, no dreams, no hopes and no heroes – good heroes, I mean. I was schooled incorrectly in Humanology. For example, I was constantly and erroneously placed into situations where I never understood things. I thought that love meant sex. I knew nothing of the soul. In return, I learned only immoral things because there was no love in my family...

As for friends, I never had many. Those I had stemmed from early childhood. Later, as I looked back I realized my life was nothing more than a great error of human development in action. One day a kid named Tony approached me at summer day camp and invited me to his house. I was twelve; he was a year younger. He wanted friendship, but his kind of friendship was bad. He sodomized and degraded me; he commanded and demanded things from me; I put up with it; I sanctioned it; I knew no better...

The experience with Tony became my lane. My path. I became a risk taker. I took risks everyday, constantly. I never stopped until *Mead* decided to stop it... Without a doubt, the only direction open to me was the wrong one. My introduction to this world of deception and peril began with this kid, and it should've never happened. But it did because we're always in the right place at the right time regardless of whether it's for something good or bad. My grandmother, Mom-Mom Ruth, told me that. She said that, one day, I would understand. Mead had a lot of tools. For instance, people who were blinded to the truth by this auxiliary power of God. Most felt sorry for really good people who were victims of tragedy, be it a fatal traffic accident or mass murder, a flash flood, tornado or a hurricane. These actions were planned and facilitated by *Mead*. The first two were carried out by *m-workers* in coordination with the *m-team*. The others were coordinated between *Mead* and *Mother Nature* and *her team*.

Since my birth I've been on autopilot, and time and again my life came face to face with trauma, which was quickly taken to heart, and burned into my central nervous system. Love? I remembered the trauma, my memory, erased any love; if there ever was any to begin with. I was the silver-ball in Mead's pinball machine, *it* bounced me around a lot.

My problem was that I was empty. There was nothing in my heart. I thought of nothing. There were no goals, no dreams, nothing. I moved through life like it was nothing. I didn't appreciate anything. I didn't hate, but I didn't love… Like I said: empty.

I was lost. Everything I did was uninhibited. My level of impulsivity was very high; I did things on whims. I feared nothing, as if there were no consequences; I didn't know what the word meant… It's the way it went. I never realized how wrong I was. I was on a path that was too wild and crazy. I never gave anything any thought. I just did whatever nefarious idea presented itself.

And then came what I described as my reckoning. The worst, hands down, was the unimaginable amount of pain from cluster headaches. So, there was hardship, but it was all well deserved. In retrospect, I knew a dozen life preservers were tossed to me over the decades. I floated upon the rough seas of trouble, but I was just like a duck who glided across a smooth pond. I suppose that I never thought that I needed help. Throughout those teenage years my conscience never worked; not even for a second. I was never violent, but my behavior was out of control. I floated atop tremendous waves that swirled around me. I was immoral, and I was immersed in mischief…

The source was *Mead* and each individual's *m-team,* which consisted of a *m-planner, m-developer, m-coordinator, m-watchers* and *m-workers. They* enveloped me from the day of my birth. Wherever I was. Whatever I did. Whatever I thought. Whatever I felt. Whatever I dreamed. Whatever I desired. Whatever I fantasized about. *M-watchers* knew it, and *m-workers* carried out *its* orders to create different paths that led me to something good, bad, or to no place at all. *They* knew the score. The data it collected never lied. *M-workers* worked in the trenches. *They* carried out *Mead* and the *m-team's* mission, in consultation with the *Executives*, which came down through the numerous levels of *its* bureaucracy.

Mead and the *m-team* were everywhere for everyone.

I was, as all were, surrounded by a vast and complex infrastructure in place just for humanity. Every other living thing was in *mother nature's* department. Each human soul was accompanied by billions of *m-workers*, who were on the job twenty-four-seven. *They* filled in every crack and crevice along the many paths that *they've* created into an individual's world: Paths related to family, friends, relationships and other encounters with random people, especially those who were different. But were they really random? *M-workers* collected an enormous amount of information. *Mead* knew everything about everybody. If someone called their boss a name behind their back, *m-watchers* took note. If someone used a slur about women, African Americans, Jews, transgender or homosexuals, *m-watchers* gauged the levels of goodness and evil. The data was so detailed that even a person's relationships with animals both wild and domestic were collected. Pathways were also critical for education, occupation, morality, goodness, and evil. Some never reached these paths, however. Some go in the wrong direction once they're on it. Some won't walk at all. They sit their way through life and they hardly ever move a muscle toward goodness or evil.

They observed and collected data on who the person really was deep inside. When it came to the leeway, however, *it* opened every dirty door. People, more often, go to jail with the kind of leeway I got. *They* dotted the I's and crossed the

T's. So intricate, these purveyors of *Mead's* monitored every second a person lived. They, constantly, collected data and channeled it back to the *m-team* and, ultimately, to *Mead*.

It was the world which existed beyond reality. *Mead* taught lessons. Throughout my youth, I never realized that I was damaged or that I wasn't well. I never knew that I was lost for decades until I understood and acknowledged *Mead*. I needed a proper education, the proper morals. I needed directions to the right path. I needed *Mead's* GPS. I never knew there were rules. I never thought about any of it. *Mead* had a plan; I was just along for the ride. I had good reason not to do any introspection. Nobody ever sat me down and had a heart to heart talk about life. I was just another kid without a father figure or a male role-model. Television and the movies provided my social education. It was as if the grown-up people around me had received orders from Mead, as it pertained to me: "Don't teach him." "Don't interact with him." "Don't intervene." "Don't love him." "Don't tolerate him," and "Don't mentor him."

And no one had. Dad stayed in the family for ten-years of my life, before he left. Even so, my memory of his presence, if not blank, was negative. One day I asked for his assistance, and he refused to give it to me. I remembered my frustration when I couldn't spell the word "of." He, in a disfatherly way, said: "I'm not going to tell you how to spell it." Much later, I realized, I had a hell of a lot of guidance and help from *Mead*. More than I ever got out of my father. However, to put this into fitness terms, *its* help focused only on strengthening my bad side. It built upon my nefarious nature, my criminal instincts, my criminology, my crimes. It kept the *m-team*, specifically, the *m-workers* and *m-watchers* busy because they had a strong work ethic, and a keen sense of morality; they knew that they were indispensable to me because those were two significant tools that I was ill equipped, and as I developed, *they* wanted to keep it that way.

I was lazy and dishonest. I never reflected on what I did, and I never stopped. As the years passed; it just got worse.

So many seasons came and went before I understood *Mead*. I wished I had gone down another path. It was there for me, but I didn't take it. I never followed any of the cues on how to live my life because I never got many… The way I saw it was that, as a result of my inability to lead a moral life, *Mead* issued instructions: "Provide paths for him to carry out all nefarious activities. Interventions non-restrictive. Deep data required…"

—

As I stood before my nephew Boris' fresh grave I looked at the great mound of red earth next to it. My thoughts never stopped: "I think too much," I complained to myself, years later. But when I learned the hierarchy of the heavens, I realized that *Mead* played too much; *it* was constantly in motion. *Mead* arranged and rearranged people's lives like furniture. At my nephew's grave site on one side there was my brother Frank, and his wife, Pat. There was also my oldest sister, Glenda, and my Uncle Stu. They were like two peas in a pod. They fed off each other like a married couple because they had so much in common. I looked at two strangers; their affections were stoic.. Each was dressed in a handsome suit.

The sky was cloudy and it looked like it wanted to rain. I felt sorry for Boris as I looked into his grave. He went the wrong way on every path he ever stood upon. But, aside from Pat, who looked sick and bereaved over his loss, the others showed disturbed expressions; they oozed angst and they looked at life as if only they possessed the truth. Their truth was filled with lies, misinformation, hatred and cruelty. Frank, Glenda and Uncle Stu, had no compassion in their eyes as they stood by the grave. My relatives looked disheartened and pathetic. Each sneered at me as I made eye contact. Their expressions told me that I had no business being there, and that I had a lotta nerve coming. I was unwelcomed. I felt their scorn. I returned their non-verbal communication with eyes of defiance. I had every right to be there, after all, I was the boy's uncle.

~~Young Sarah~~ F stared blankly at the coffin as it was lowered into the ground. Pat pulled her closer to her. She was a good mom, but she drank too much, Frank once told me. She also broke her foot, which initiated her addiction to Rich Pliartrum's painkillers.

Pliartrum's opioids have killed nearly one-hundred-thousand people every year, even before he became President of the United States. He outdid himself with the pandemic; it was reported that a million people died as a result of his so-called leadership. His pain clinics and retreats dot the world's landscape, although, primarily, in the United States. He was a television stooge who fed his ego every week with thoughts of power and great wealth on a reality show, which determined if someone who was fat was sexy. He insulted and degraded them, each week, as he spent the hour clearing his clogged ego.

I stood motionless. Nearby, I watched a crow who pecked the ground for food; it reminded me that I pecked at *Mead's* door a great deal. Once I realized it I was curious about the special power. I knew nothing about *its* motive…. Why pit brother against brother, again and again, over countless centuries?

—

 I offered an expression that communicated that I felt sorry for my relatives across the grave. Each, individually, nodded and repaid me with their disdain and animosity. It was as if it came from a bunch of thugs, Pliartrum's thievery, which was like no others. And the psychosis; it was all too surreal. How does someone fall victim to this, I asked myself?The mass psychosis spread through country-clubs and Bubba's place of worship. It paralleled Nazi Germany; it couldn't be clearer. The World has, once again, flipped. It had lost its mind. Most individuals, who succumbed to, fed on and gained power through Pliartrum's hatred and cruelty. The split modeled World War II because history always repeated itself. Again, courtesy of *Mead*...

Mead processed roughly two-hundred-thousand humans who were brought into this world, and four-hundred-thousand humans who had reached their expiration date on any given day. Mankind's conception, and the entirety of *Mead* was hard for me to process at first. *Mead* took care of everything – All the details and intricacy from the moment of birth; through the magic of childhood; the uneasiness of teenagehood; the depression or enlightenment of the twenties; the highs and lows of the thirties; the seriousness of the forties; the stocktaking of the fifties; the reckoning of the sixties; the stark reality of the seventies. Add all of humanity's daily functionality; its intercourse, its direction, its milliseconds of interplay between soul, self, and *Mead*. God and the *Executives* were busy with more pressing matters than the management of humans. *Mead's* priorities focused on each level of an individual's life. It began with the soul and self. Then family and friends. Finally, the neighbors, co-workers, supervisors along with our interactions with strangers. People who passed by. Those who we've bumped into or met. People we've served. People who've served us. Each, unbeknownst to one another. The intricacy *it* took to arrange it...The sensitivity of the data... The hate and the harm *it* caused... *It's* sabotage between inner-self and the physical-self... *Its* interactions with others. *Its* tool of solitude. *Its* armies of *m-workers*, who generated battles, delivered pain and torture, abuse and neglect, and the demise of an individual within itself. Within its family. Within its relations. Within every facet of life. *Mead* had it all covered.

The knowledge hit me. God doesn't have the time to attend to eight-billion people. And, anyone who ever put any thought to it, the World, required more than angels who interceded when a terrible wrong had occurred. Nor, the demons. Supervisors of hate, violence; even murder.

Mead and the *m-team's* major duty; *it* identified conflict, and created pivotal moments in a person's daily lives. It was maintained and built upon. Pressure mounted. Boiling points were reached between genders, brothers and other family members. Neighbors were no longer tolerated. A person's sexual orientation or transgender individuals were, once again, an issue. These were all distractions, however, because *Mead* tested, besides the individual, family, friends and co-workers, communities, nations, races and religions; conflicts in the World since the dawn of time.

M-workers who oversaw each individual, and their interactions within their daily world, focused, family, relationships, or the lack of. *It* worked in homeless shelters and country- clubs, prisons and beaches. In hospitals and morgues. Garbage dumps, strip joints. Pharmacies, factories. Be it Portland to Peking or Moscow to Tokyo; *Mead* worked on everything down to minutest detail, immersed in everything, at any time; anywhere. Everything that took place in the day to day lives of the humans on earth; it was all *Mead*. All of the good and all the bad. All of the boredom and the thrills. No matter who. No matter where. No matter when. No matter what; it's all coordinated. Each human was integrated into its system. It started at the moment of conception, which was all prearranged by *Mead*. Sometimes it's a planned abortion. Sometimes the baby was unwanted. Sometimes it's a planned date of birth. Sometimes it's the individual's upcoming expiration date.

Plainly put, *Mead* was a paramount and a juggernaut; an unimaginable system, which performed unimaginable feats. *It* was magical. *It* set the parameters. *It* provided pathways. Sometimes, it's so random. People who are born into a life of poverty, filled with hunger, squalor and decay. It could be to live a life filled with joy, goodness and integrity. Or those hooked on destruction through their addictions, to alcohol, heroin, fentanyl or methamphetamine.

Mead never did things without a reason. A lesson always existed; however, it was seldom learned. Every since time was, within each and every century of mankind's existence, *Mead* liked to shake things up. To turn everything on its head. It happened time and again, and whenever it occurred people wore blinders provided by the *m-workers* at the behest of those above. Right becomes wrong, and wrong becomes right. Truth becomes a lie, and lies becomes the truth. Up is down, and down is up. The whole world had gone mad; yet again. Brothers at each other's throats. These divided individuals and their communities faced *Mead's* scrutiny. Data was collected on conflicts over race, religion and politics. I knew that this time the entire world was in conflict. The future of America rested on the shoulders of those who were not caught up in the shared-psychosis of the Country Club Party. As the clock ticked away, *Mead's* lessons to humanity, once again, won't be realized.

For some, when the party was over, a small fraction of each group-type, when it comes to good and evil, couldn't predict their demise, they've reached their expiration date but they had no clue. A victim of murder or an accident; it was *Mead's* territory. In other cases it's a bolt of lightning; a fiery car crash in the middle of a hail storm. Earthquakes, landslides, sinkholes, tornados, flash floods, wildfires, rock slides, hurricanes, even bee stings. *They* all accomplished *their* tasks thanks to the collaboration and coordination of *Mead's m-team* along with *Mother Nature's mn-workers*.

Chapter 2

As I watched the wooden coffin of my nephew's casket being lowered into the ground; emotionally, I was as empty as a football. My only thought being what a cheap casket they put him in.

Boris was always in trouble. He once told me that he always gets caught. He was right, he always did; time after time. From his childhood into his teenage years he faced trouble with the law. *Mead* had him in and out of the clinker so often; it truly was a door that revolved until the end; his expiration date. Now, no more jail cells for Boris...

My eyes moved to my niece's grave, Sarah. She appeared to me in my mind's eye. She was a shy and serious child, and with her glasses on she looked very studious. She studied a lot and did well in school. She had a really-good friend, which she was one as well. She loved to read and write poetry. She would've gone far. As Boris' younger sister, and Frank and Pat's daughter she made the family a family, in my eyes. Her grave was dug not very long ago. She's proof, I thought, that *Mead* existed... Next, I looked at my mother's headstone; it sat next to one of my older sisters, Lily. All four graves were each less than a year old. There were other empty plots. But, I thought, it was no place for me. Absolutely, no one would be in attendance. Nobody would stand over my grave. There were people who wished for my demise, my oldest sister, Glenda, for one. She was present when Mom was put to rest. She was crazy after the funeral. As soon as we got to Mom's house she hurried up the stairs to her bedroom there was desperation in her voice when she said: *"Where's that three-hundred-dollar sweater I bought her in Paris?"* She was in Mom's will. She was already a multi-millionaire, so fifteen-thousand-dollars, from Mom's will, was nothing to her. But she wanted more; it was never enough for her. Once she threw a fit. She implicated me. I was responsible because she was forced to cough up fifteen-dollars for a cab ride.

Boris' grave sat near to the intersection where Mom and Lily were buried; it was just a stone's throw away from my maternal grandparents Mom-Mom and Pop-Pop, who each received a large send-off. Many people came to the cemetery when Mom passed away too; one-hundred-and-thirty-nine souls signed the book. As for Lily, my sweet sister, there were over three-hundred in attendance…

Glenda, my sour sister, was a force in any arrangement she found herself in. She was as cold as dry ice. She did a lot of damage too; she didn't care who she stepped on. My, unscrupulous, sibling charmed people the way an unsavory preacher preached to his God fearing congregation when the hat was passed around; she hoodwinked them.

On the other hand, my beloved sister, Lily, had a very rich life filled with the ingredients necessary for its optimal function. She had an abundance of goodness in her. She earned the love and respect of others through her pleasant eyes and warm personality. But she was smart, too. People admired Lily. She admired people, all kinds of people. Diversity Lily, they called her. She conducted her life effortlessly. Her ability to warm somebody's heart. Her sincerity. She kept that alive all of her life. At least, it was the way I saw her as I grew older. Glenda was a witch, and Lily was an angel. My wicked sister sucked donkey dicks, I used to say to myself. But my good sister proved to be a mighty adversary…

———

I guess I formed my overall opinion of my sisters early in life when Mom-Mom told me a story about them. We were alone at the time. It was night and I remembered that the room felt very still and quiet. I didn't hear a thing except her voice. I burned every word into my memory. She told me that something happened to Lily when I was just a toddler. Dad had taken the girls to the *Farm Show*, for the harvest festival. It was a cool autumn night; sweatshirt weather. Both girls grabbed hold of one of Dad's hands as they made their way through the parking lot towards the Farm Show Building. They looked around for a while. When dad stopped to talk to a salesman, Glenda and Lily wandered to the little chicks exhibit. There were dozens of the tiny feathered birds in an empty kiddy-pool. Little yellow chicks, as innocent as ladybugs, Mom-Mom said that Lily had picked up a chick and held it. Glenda picked one up too and she closed her hands around it and squeezed it for a minute. Lily watched in horror as Glenda held her arms out like two-minutes, and opened her hands. The chick was dead. She had smothered it. She suffocated it. She squeezed it to death. Then, to add to trauma to the tragedy; she dangled the dead little chick upside down in front of Lily's face. Later, when Dad found out he scolded Glenda. It damaged Lily.

Mead watched children, particularly when they acted out. It was his prelude, his coming attraction. A prompt to stay tuned; there's more to see. My oldest sister, the psychopath, never killed anybody, yet. But *Mead* controlled her too. It enabled her. It gave her pathways. It arranged who she encountered. Her life changing events. Its trajectory damaged society. Goodness created and built it. Evil destroyed it and burned it down. Goodness built it all back up. Evil burned it back down…

Lily never made decisions lightly. She knew of a sweet young child named Manuel, who bounced around the foster care system. She learned about him from a foster care provider who came to her pottery school. She thought about the boy and his future for months before her maternal instincts helped her decide to bring him into her life by adopting him. Her decision did not surprise me. I figured that she would plunge headlong into raising Manuel with as much fervor as she had for politics and world affairs. I recalled at dinner one night when I was young, Lily talked about a girl at school who was a foster child. She felt sorry for her, she later told me, because she never had a real mom and dad. When Lily said that she wanted to be a foster parent one day, Glenda raised her eyebrow and laughed.

But, later in life, when she carried out what she wished, it would prove consequential. Lily had never been a parent. And our parenting was poor. She told me she believed if she gave the boy all the time and attention that he needed he'd be okay. She quickly learned it was not an option anymore. Manuel had been a handful all of his life. What she didn't know was that the adoption played out the way it was supposed to turn out. The pottery student provided the prompt. *Mead* and the *m-team* did the rest.

They coordinated everything. All the right parties at all the right times in all the right places came together to change lives. A shift of a human's tectonic plates altered many lives; it was all just another day's work for *Mead* and the *m-planners, m-developers, m- coordinators* and the *m-watchers* and *m-workers*.

I reached down and picked a dandelion weed out of the ground; it laid upon Lily's grave. I remembered how she glowed. She looked like an angel. Her eyes were always comforting. She cared and it came through. Her whole being spoke. She always handed out comfort words; tender words. Words that made someone think. She was casual to the eye, but that was part of her persona. She was contagious, and when there was a crisis or a problem people turned to her. She wasn't just a really good woman. She was very wise too. She rarely made any mistakes…

Mom, on the other hand, was quite the opposite. She was left to raise four-children alone. She tried her best after Dad ran off with another woman. The lady was twelve-years younger than him. *Mead* broke Mom and split up the family. A frenzy ensued. Lives turned upside down. We kids were confused. We each acted-out in some fashion. I was non-compliant. Lily rarely spoke. Glenda went violent. One day she smacked little Frank across the face for saying something stupid that she took offense to. All I saw out of that sister was her bad side.

  Life was in perpetual motion; it changed all the time. That was one of *Mead's* specialties: i*t* broke everything. *It* destroyed a person's world. Their marriages, romances, friendships met with scrutiny and conflict, and that same person was watched and tested. Data was collected that showed how they managed. All of the developments. The good, bad or indifferent. The *m-team* stayed on it. The data monitored every split second. Every minute of every hour. Every day, they collected an enormous amount. It reported who did what. And who didn't. Who made things better? Who made things worse? Who dealt with it? M-workers collected data on how people got along with themselves and others. It kept track of family interplay. It monitored people at work. M-workers tracked relations with their peers at school, and at play; it even happened at a hospital to gauge whether or not the person valued life.

  Mead kept Mom on a tightrope.

She voluntarily admitted herself into the psychiatric ward in the same hospital where Glenda, Lily, Frank and I were born. She checked herself out a day after her admission; she picked herself up and moved on; it was tough on her and us kids. We split as a family; everyone went their separate ways.

I stared at her gravestone and I recalled that Mom was ill-prepared for her own life. She graduated from high school, but she never worked anywhere. She was a housewife. But, after the divorce she got her life together. She got a job in a low skilled position at a doctor's office. We were clothed. A roof was always over our heads. And there was always a floor beneath us and food in our bellies. Dad married Ellen in 1968, when I was ten. I had no memories of him when he was in the family prior to when he left; it was like he was never there.

I never realized that I had no connection to anyone in my immediate family until I became an adult. I was close to my Mom-Mom, she showed her goodness to me; something others refused to do, didn't know how to do, or just preferred not to do. In turn, later, I realized that I refused to show mine as a result. But when I looked back I saw that I showed it, sometimes. What I remembered most about Mom-Mom was how she showed her goodness even if she was being serious. She never got mad. She showed it even when she was being strict. She taught me about goodness, but I buried it deep inside me; it was years before I brought it out and used it…

My grandparents' graves were nearby. As I passed by them, earlier, my memory shot back to those early years; suddenly, I looked away because I felt ashamed. My family members eventually merged into other families, which meant I was minus a family. When I got older, and when I was on my own, I realized a family never existed in the first place. To me the word family was just a word. I knew nothing of it. I never had a normal healthy human interaction, a friendship or a relationship. I was void of honesty and trustworthiness.

Chapter 3

A graveyard was an appropriate spot for the first gathering of Glenda, Frank and Uncle Stu and me again, because our relations were dead. My late sister Lily stirred the political pot of the nation. I stood by her until her expiration date. After that I maintained Lily's fever. We were all close in proximity but so far away, otherwise. I thought, today, my presence would be a conciliatory gesture to meet half-way. To come to some kind of an understanding, but it never happened. I shook my head to break the thought and I realized that I never focused on Boris' or his path in life… He was so different. I had difficulty relating to him as an uncle. My uncle's were scattered across the land, and I rarely saw any of them. But, as his uncle and my experiences in mental health I saw that his antisocial behavior had no bounds. I recalled that Pat once told me that, as a child, he was fascinated with birds; he wished he was born a vulture.

I pulled two tissues out of my pocket. Lily's headstone had bird poop on it. I spit into one of the tissues and wiped it off. I stepped back and I gazed at her headstone: *Lily Issacs 1955-2022 Beloved by All*. I used the other throwaway rag to wipe away a tear.

Lily never married. Her romance never blossomed. The really good guy she was very close to was killed along with seven others at a McDonalds, in Seattle. I lacked emotion when I learned that Lily wasn't with him because it happened so much in this country. The boyfriend and seven others were in the establishment at the time; it was just another random mass murder in the United States of America. But after she was murdered, too, I recognized that *Mead* had a place for all. A place for the good. A place for the not so good. A place for the bad. A place for the not so bad. Finally, there was a place, set aside, for the just plain evil.

After the death of her friend, Lily's life shifted slightly. She began to focus on the world around her more fervently, especially the political arena. One day, while shopping at the local mall for sneakers for Manuel, she saw a new path open for her. She had always been slightly politically active, but now, on this day, she suddenly became passionate.

A friend intercepted her at the mall and together they expressed their activism by handing out leaflets that focused on the People Party. Her whole world was caught up in a ludicrous frenzy over former President Rich Pliartrum, and what he did to the United States. Before he became president, Pliartrum, had a twelve-year run as a successful daytime talk show advice giver. He took over his father's company, and was the driving force of big-pharma. He was responsible for the success of *Axalt*, a powerful and addictive painkiller. His company was found liable and he was forced to pay litigants who sued him over his actions before he was president, as he was president, and after he left the presidency. *Axalt* became the least of his crimes...

I sat at Lily's computer after she was gone. I watched videos she and her political buddy exchanged. I looked at photos of them together, travel photos; childhood pictures; it all felt very intimate and tender; it touched me. I was sensitive to it. I gently pressed each key as I searched; it was as if I was in slow motion. I peeked into their personal worlds. Each shared their highs and lows. They exposed their hearts to one another. They shared moments of success and triumph. Their tiresome tribulations and failures painted a portrait too. I read more than a hundred emails, which Lily exchanged with her friend. Some of it deeply touched me. One really pissed me off.

I learned that Glenda had invited Lily to Manhattan for a weekend. Glenda was hideous to her. She shamed my younger sister over her fervent support to stop Pliartrum and his politics. My famous sister tended to a small group at a cocktail party in her penthouse. Lily was way out of place. Her life lacked the glamor she saw that night. Glenda had the nerve to introduce Lily as "her sister who eats at *McDonalds*." She thought it was hilarious. Lily felt emotional, she wrote, because her boyfriend was killed in one.

I called her up, and, afterwards, I lost my access to her; she blocked my calls ever since I read Lily's words to her. My eldest sister deserved it. I said to her that I prayed that she rotted in hell for her lack of scruples. I understood as well. I leaned back in her office chair and thought that Glenda and I were a lot alike, actually. I led an early life with no scruples. My goodness remained invisible, so no one ever saw it. Nothing I did was personal in nature. "It was just business," as I recalled the line from *The Godfather*.

I guess I was beginning to get a deeper understanding of life after Boris' death, a wave of clarity washed over me . Everything, including death, was set up in advance by *Mead*.

Mead was never called upon. *It* acted when *it* acted. That is, if *it* acted at all; *it* decided what mattered; the fate of every human. The end of each life. Each soul's designated expiration date was preset. The day and the time; the place and the manner. What should've it been? Suicide due to poor health. A traffic accident. A slip on a sheet of ice. A fall down a flight of stairs. Or was it the end of a life that walked on a darkened path. An experience that yearned in the heart. A homicidal rage or an act rooted in passion and love. A mass murderer who sought power through hate. Or was it another sick kid, defiled by a sick society. The young eyes were traumatized without warning; without counsel. It subjected a young mind to the horrible world of evil before it ever had the chance to realize their wonderful world of goodness.

With my oldest sister's help I became curious. A neighbor kid and I got hold of a tobacco pipe. We smoked it and nothing happened. We both looked at each other and we shrugged our shoulders. I don't know why Glenda left that envelope and even though the pot did not seem to affect me, I had never forgotten about it. I was a mere thirteen-year-old.

I walked away from it for years, and then it was reintroduced to me. This time the high hit me. I was at the age of fifteen. On Saturday nights, I played poker and a joint was passed around. Suddenly, for the first time, I was high; it was the most historic day of my life. I never drank alcohol; a wicked tool in *Mead's* trade. I just smoked. I didn't want alcohol. I understood, later, that I defied *Mead*. Someone like me usually drank to death. They committed crimes and were incarcerated or took their own life. I didn't do any of those things. I smoked, period. I was spared. My fate was undetermined. Why, I'm not sure. I needed a lot of work done. I needed constant supervision. I was rebellious. I played by different rules, my own, and I had a knack. I pressed people's buttons; somehow, I reached Mead.

My teens were the most unconstructive period in my life. Years when my young soul learned nothing. The flightless bird was not prepared to fly. Adulthood awaited. Someone readied. A person who contributed a mind, a body and a soul. Be it good or bad or of no consequence at all. I was still a kid inside. but I never faced it…

Sometimes, I imagine myself as I read book after book. I studied, did homework and learned how to grow physically, mentally and socially. I was socially retarded, however, which was how I saw myself later in life. At the time, however, I had no clue what I was doing and what I wasn't doing. I grew physically but I was never in shape. I never made any effort toward any goal so that I lived a healthy life. I never ate right. I never exercised. I never practiced good tighter grip with cannabis. I looked down upon those coldblooded creatures, and I spat on them.

The clusters, as I referred to them, were sometimes as precise as a timeclock. Each day, at a precise time, an evil and sadistic pair came to dine on my brain and one of my eyes. They feasted on me. They used utensils that agonized and debilitated me. An icepick stabbed and grinded the eye. It pounded as it pulsated. It was relentless, level-ten pain. It was so severe it became lethal to some. Few of the ignorant prevailed; many took their own lives. I had no clue as to how to combat it. I agonized over the tortured punishment. I never knew why. Neoroligists never knew why. Only Mead knew. I simply endured the pain and agony, day and night for decades. Until, I gained the upper hand… It all started when Mead decided when and where I was to be introduced to illegal drugs and *it* did it through my evil sister.

Glenda introduced me to cannabis the morning she went off to college. I was thirteen and Frank was eight. We shared a room. There were two identical beds, nightstands and dresser drawers. I remembered I was still in bed when Glenda entered my room. I was sleepy eyed; but I saw that she opened the top drawer of my dresser, and put an envelope in it. She closed the drawer, and walked out and said nothing. Later, I got out of my bed, which I peed in again, and I retrieved the envelope. On it she wrote *"Have Fun."* She'd never shown an interest in me before, as I remembered. I looked at the envelope; it had in it something other than paper. I shook it. Honest to God, up to that point, I never did drugs. I never knew anything about them. I was still a young kid. My school never educated us about it back then, so it was never on my radar screen. I never thought about or even uttered the word, marijuana. It was unknown to me what it did or that it even existed.

oral hygiene. I only damaged myself because I had only to go to school, go to work after school, and to get high. No homework, no study sessions; no workouts or sports, nothing. Nothing deviated me from my nightly ritual. I escaped from the world; consequently, I prepared for nothing.

In adulthood, I didn't smoke all the time; it wasn't until after I got off of work. All my free time.was devoted to it, however. Since I never drank alcohol; its availability and access never mattered. I hated the shit. At any time, cannabis or not, I never drank. It was only marijuana that I wanted, but she played hard to get.

I was a senior and retired before I fully realized that *Mead* had me covered ever since childhood. Over those years, I never questioned anything; it just happened. I just carried on. My behaviors never changed. Night after night, day after day; month after month and year after year, until I graduated high-school…

Much later, I understood these interventions were too fantastic. I had never wondered or thought about it. I had never acknowledged it either because I had no awareness of *it*. I never stopped. I continued until *it* stopped me. I was placed on another path. It was one which was dark, painful and isolated…

My life was prepared to accomplish everything I put an effort into up to that point, which was absolutely nothing. I had bizarre, untamed, unwanted; unbelievable experiences… I had the ability to go on like nothing ever happened. I was a kid; life just continued. My thoughts were on automatic pilot. I never talked about my affairs, which is another display of Mead's power because a lot of times, I won't shut up.

My actions were never planned. I acted on impulse. I stole money. Each day, I stuffed my pockets with cash. It was back when there were no UPC codes or scanners; it was just a simple cash register. I was without a conscience, and I felt nothing. I continued and I never thought about the consequences. I never thought or was in any way worried that I'd be caught. I came close. I should've been caught a couple of times, when the police should've been called, and that I should've been searched; it should've stopped me. There were so many other times it should've happened, but it never did…

I never thought about it. It happened so many times that my life should've been ruined. I tried to ruin it myself, but *Mead* had different plans for me… Up to that point my deeds were bad. I was glad that I never told anyone a word about my criminality. It was really *Mead* who shutted me up. I deserved being caught. I never got caught, as an adult I wondered why? As a teen it never entered my mind. Why was I spared the ins and outs of prison? Why were others left to rot? Why was I permitted to go on?

I had never improved either physically or mentally. I never learned about life. I never grew emotionally. I never planned except for nefarious purposes, and it was always on a whim. I never had any goals. I had no virtue, no morality. I was a human being void of humanity. I earned money from my job but, otherwise, all I had was dirty money. It fed my addiction to thoroughbreds at the racetrack; something Uncle Stu introduced me to at age sixteen. He was in his thirties. He paid my way into the clubhouse and gave me money to bet; it was my only contact with him. He never had anything else to do with me. Later, I realized that *Mead* set him up to introduce me to it because, immediately, I was hooked.

Every night after work I took the money I stole and I pissed it away on the ponies. It was my world. No friends or romance.

No vision or awareness. No morality. Absolutely nothing happened to me. No consequences. No juvenile detention center. No counselors. No nurses. No doctors. No program technicians. No isolation. No restraints… I was educated. Just by other means…

I possessed two positive traits. Surprisingly, my empathy and compassion toward unfortunate people surfaced. Businesses were another matter. I guessed that *Mead* saw it in me. It was my teenage existence. I stole at every opportunity. I gave items away; they weren't mine to give. I was a mindless person. It's why, sometimes, I struggled with the belief that life wasn't real. Because when I looked back it seemed like it was an episode of the *Twilight Zone*.

Chapter 5

Frank and Pat met at the local American Legion, VFW #322. She was a bartender and he was a customer. The club was private. Only VFW members, their spouses and their guests were admitted. She drank and smoked while she worked. "I must," she said. Fumes of alcohol and smoke triggered what she wanted, and at the VFW, it was allowed.

Before that she attended the community college in our hometown. She received an associate's degree in Criminal Justice. She planned to earn her Master's Degree. She dreamt that she worked for the FBI, in their criminal division. She wanted to specialize in forensics. She worked hard and earned top grades. She was well on her way to where she realized her goals and her fantasies. But a momentous event dashed it all. She stopped her job search. She gave it all up just two days before graduation. She never attended the graduation ceremony. Her life shifted away from her dreams.

She was placed on a different path. She lived another life. Instantly, when it happened, her mind told her that she was done. Her subconscious mind, overseen by *Mead* and operated by the *m-team*, searched her data and her profile for alternatives to her future. She panicked; the panic turned to despair. She wanted a drink. She moved far away in her mind. She freed herself, and at that moment she flew away like a bird. She never got off the ground, however. She resigned herself to the consequences of the moment. She changed her plans. She immersed herself into her second favorite area of interest… She wondered, just for a few seconds, what it was like, and how she'd much rather be somewhere else at that moment. But, there she was, naked for all to see. She and two of her girlfriends were arrested.

She had only smoked it a couple of times. She told me that she never really liked it. There was none found on her person when she was frisked, but she was arrested nonetheless. She had been a passenger in a car; the inside of which wreaked from the smell of cannabis. Each occupant was charged. A campus police officer had pinched the trio quite unexpectedly. He was only on duty for a few minutes, he said. Suddenly, the car whizzed by. He followed it and he noticed that the car's movement became somewhat erratic. He pulled the car over. That moment triggered a major shift for Pat. Life challenged her as she walked on her path. She was thrown off kilter. Her dreams, fantasies, hopes and desires were all dashed forever; it all happened simultaneously.

It changed the trajectory of her life. She never sought further education in the field she studied. She never applied for any of the dream positions she aspired to for so long. She had no motivation. She never hung in there. She fought the consequences. She never launched a battle for redemption. Instantaneously, she knew her future was unattainable, and it was all because, as her father said, she was in the wrong place at the wrong time. But, the more I thought about it I became convinced that she was in the right place at the right time. The *m-watchers* and *m-workers* acted. *They* forged a new and different path for her. *They* did *their* job. *They* facilitated the conflict within herself. She was thrown off her course. She never fought for what she wanted. She never succeeded.

Back then, few humans instantaneously realized and attained their goals without a fight from *Mead* and the *m-team*. Each attribute in the person's data was weighed. The healthy versus the positive. If a discrepancy occurred, for instance, whether or not they were pitted against the other. It worked out any contradictions within each of us. For those it did not work out, they were doomed to remain stuck in the mud of life.

All of a person's tone in voice and manner, including their morality, their decency, their deeds in life, are weighed and considered; the good, bad or indifferent. Were they good or evil? People who built and healed rather than those who burned and destroyed. The subject was one step closer to what it yearned for so deeply inside. A fantasy, a dream, a desire to realize the unattainable, the unimaginable. The essence of what was in someone's heart. It constantly tested our place in society. It led us, ultimately, whether we liked it or not, to where *Mead* had planned for it to go.

Sometimes, however, it was seemingly impossible for the individuals to make any headway. They tried. They fought. They worked hard. But they went nowhere because their data never showed a tendency of movement toward either polar. The area of our being. It lurked within the catacombs of the mind. For the majority, it looked like plaque, decay or tartar. It was piled on a set of weary teeth over a long period of time. But, those problems were in the mind. Not one that was oral in nature.

From the very top to the bottom. All pivotal moments an individual chooses, mindful or not, are recorded. I did something good for someone or I did something which tormented, hazed or belittled them. From something kind and thoughtful to something hurtful and hateful. From the peaceful and soulful to the ravages of conflict and war. Was it something moral or was it filled with immorality?

Pat's entire life changed. She was turned upside down. It was all due to the *m-workers*. She told the campus police officer, before she got in the car, that she never knew that they smoked marijuana, even though she admitted that she smoked it with them before. She spent the rest of the day in custody. She was released to her father later. She was fined and placed on probation for a year, which she spent at home. She drank alcohol and sulked over her woes. She hid from herself.

While on probation she moved into an apartment in another town. She attended a vocational school, and got a certificate in bartending. She worked in the field there for two-years, before she decided she wanted to move back home. Nearer to her mother and father, a comfort that she always acknowledged, she told Frank that she missed how her parents always smiled. That they hugged and kissed each other on the cheek, all of the time, especially coming and going.

Pat's folks lived in Patriot Park. It was a small township, which housed the area's biggest location where people shopped. The Patriot Park Mall it was called, and it was located up the street from VFW American Legion, which was just a half a mile away from Pat's childhood home. She moved back in with her parents; her mother was a sweet blabbermouth who meant no harm but she had an almost constant homespun monologue of knowledge. She loved to talk. She rarely listened. She'd talk about anything and everything for as long as she wanted. The patient husband, Pat's father, was a well respected man. He served full-time as a one-star General, in the *National Guard* for thirty-years. George rarely interrupted Dorothy. He kept himself occupied. He read the newspaper, books, magazines, cereal boxes, anything. I thought that it distracted or protected him from her almost constant flow of speech. She was always filled with goodness, however. She wasn't a woman to use cross words or to say something bad about anyone.

In the twentieth-century, the Atwill family moved into their dream suburban home. The young couple with two young children flourished in their new surroundings. It became the most popular house in the suburban neighborhood. Its location was racially and religiously segregated. It sat in the white, anglo-saxon section of town. Black folks lived in another jurisdiction. Jewish people made their homes elsewhere, as well.

Every room, above ground, in Pat's childhood home, was small. Their kitchen, its three- bedrooms and two bathrooms were all cramped. The living and dining rooms had more leg room. It boasted, however, that it had a large finished basement and was patronized by many neighbors, relatives and friends on a regular basis. It was due to the family's hospitality as well as their social skills, and the presence of a large built-in swimming pool in the backyard. It even had a diving board. The whole thing was a rarity in a northeastern state. Other attractions of the home included a large concrete patio for people to congregate. There were lawn chairs, and two picnic tables nearby, where families ate grilled chicken. Inside there were people who congregated. Their murmured voices were drowned out only by a raucous laugh. Cigarette smoke hung in the air. Cheerful and carefree, they kibitzed by an authentic bar table with a half dozen barstools.

The bar was fully stocked. It boasted a sink, and a large collection of alcohol related memorabilia. Neon-beer signs, a giant statue of a hobo who leaned against a post holding a bottle, and a huge lamp shaped like a whiskey bottle; it was labeled.

Blue skies, with a bright hot sun, mercilessly beat down on the surface of the water, it created a glimmered affect to those gathered inside.

"If it's the dead of summer, and a weekend, added to a humid afternoon, then the basement and pool are a blessing," Pat's Mom said. They all sported swimsuits, shorts, t-shirts, flip-flops and sandals. Most of the adults smoked as they nursed bottles of beer, glasses of wine, shots of whiskey and various mixed drinks. Those were the happy days; the alcohol flowed very freely; it was always a good time. Pat was a very popular child. She was smart and outgoing. She inherited her mother's gift for gab. The grown-ups smiled and laughed at her when she sweetly interrupted their smalltalk. She wanted a sip of their alcoholic drink. The adults were amused as the young girl raised her eyebrows as she brightened her eyes and sipped it. So, I learned how it all started for her. She just sipped in her early years but she had her first real drink by the age of twelve.

Her marriage to Frank coincided with the retirement of her father. After tireless work for the National Guard all of those years, he bought a top of the line motorhome, and with his wife, traveled all over the country.

It all worked out great for Frank. Pat's family sold their dream home to him and his new bride. The new couple now lived in the house she grew up in. Frank was into it too. He felt the love and closeness when Pat brought him home to meet her mother and father. They played *Uno*. Frank never experienced this type of family connection. But after he experienced it he sought it out more, and soon, he thrived on it. It was a happy period for him..

Frank earned his bachelor's degree. He was hired by the County to collect property taxes.The family was relatively stable. One day, that Pat always recalled, was when she was a girl and her mother placed a wooden step stool in front of the sink. Pat looked excited as she stood upon it. "Look, Mommy, I can see real good now." As her mother, she said, pointed to different things. One of them was "the pretty lady in the window." All was well, and they flourished. Pat drank nothing but water when she had Boris, who was born three months after they married.

Boris entered the world on a cold and blustery day. Pat tended to him more than Frank, but that was only in the beginning. Once he learned to walk he was in constant motion. So, the day he wanted to look out of the kitchen window to see the birds, Pat retrieved a small wooden stool from the garage, which was where it was stored for decades. Pat told Boris the story of the stool, and he stepped up on it. He was stimulated by it. He stood on his tippy-toes to see more. Pat pointed things out to the little guy, just like her mother did when she was his age. Suddenly, she appeared. "Look, it's the pretty woman in the window, now she's an old lady," The mother told her son that she had seen her since she was a girl his age.

Later, when she had Sarah she did the same thing. It was a happy family, but, later, it was fueled by alcohol, because once Pat started to drink again, it became the family's Achilles heel. Later, her Pliartrum pharmaceutical drug addiction began. She had an accident and her injury infected her entire foot, which was broken. That's when the pain medication moved in. A year later Frank became a volunteer for the Country Club Party. He made connections and found people that he had a lot in common with. They believed that the nation's populations were infected and changes were necessary. They saw it as a white man's problem, and they had a way to solve it. They tolerated no one. They demonized and degraded others different from themselves. They were intoxicated by the year's presidential election. Their candidate won. He had the same attitudes and beliefs as them, and he poured more fuel on the fire because newly elected President Rich Pliartrum, was an arsonist.

Chapter 6

I never stopped. I stole mercilessly. It was ingrained in me. There was an incident when I was very young that I remembered. We visited our cousins in New York, and we all went to the New York World's Fair. We had lunch. When we left I recalled that Dad told Mom that he never paid for the food. They both smirked, smiled and shrugged their shoulders. It sent a nefarious message to me. It began a phase when I practiced my thievery, and I felt good about it.

I left the retail sector when I became a senior in high school. I found another part time job. This time my angel face landed a job at a drugstore. I delivered prescription drugs. Well, at least, I delivered most of them. My thievery reached new heights, but I felt no shame, no guilt, nothing.

It was the early 1970s, the loosest and most decadent decade in the latter half of the Twentieth-Century. We had a president who was forced to resign because of his moral haywire compass. We had movies like *The Godfather*, and *Godfather II*. It glorified crime, and was a big influence on me. I never knew why, except to say that I acted them out, but in real time. I took tremendous risks, minus any violence. But I was absolutely oblivious to any consequences. It never fazed me. Later in life, when I found my sanity, it did. I had gone about my mindless days as if I had no moral leadership in my life to follow because I didn't. There was no real person that I looked up to or who I emulated. I was satisfied with my every whim. If I wanted something, just as if I were a young child, I did whatever it took to get it.

The *JCC* was a haven that I walked a mile to get to. It was a half mile up and a half mile back. I was always happy to go there. It got me away from Mom and Glenda and vice-versa; it was a regular goal of theirs and mine. They wanted me around as little as possible. Being around them always made me nauseous sometimes. But for an eleven-year-old it was hard not to see them. I was only away from them in the summer and when I was in school or when I walked to and from the center. I was mostly alone there. I was always by myself. No other Jewish kids, my age, hung out there. I played racquetball and I bowled with a childhood friend, but that was it.

Lily on the other hand participated. I didn't see her as much as I saw Glenda. My youngest sister was very popular and she was always going somewhere, or was doing something. Before the age of ten, she was quiet and reserved. After her tenth-birthday she was on the swim team. I watched her races. She also volunteered to work at the library. She put books back in their proper places on the shelf. But mostly she sat and talked with the adult librarians. She later recounted that they made her feel that they enjoyed having her around. She babysat a lot too. A lot more than Glenda, who only did it when it was for rich people who paid top dollar. They wanted someone with "my beauty and sophistication," she once told Mom. She met and knew many rich people due to her social connections. It included regular excursions to a country club. A girlfriend, from a rich family, took her numerous times in the summer to "lay by the pool." She laid there all right. She looked great in a swimsuit with her skin bronzed. She looked rich so she acted rich. She worked the circuit like she had been a part of it all her life. She went to parties and wedding receptions. She played tennis and golfed. She was eye candy to the golf-pro, she told her friend: "He offered her private lessons."

As for me, even though I had no friends, I always tried to get along with everyone that I encountered. As I looked back, I wanted to please people. When I was young I sought people's attention and approval. Being liked and agreeable to others was always forefront in my mind.

I never was in a physical fight. I never clenched my fist in anger, or raised my hand to my mother or anybody else, for that matter. I was a passive thief. Scruples be damned.

So, what in the hell happened? To put it plainly, I screwed up. However, I was never caught in the act. I was to go unpunished for decades… Up until then I still waded peacefully in *Mead's* ocean. I tiptoed through grade school. I passed, but I never applied myself, except for when there was a written assignment, which I excelled at.

As to my socialization, I wasn't aware of my predicament. The fact was that I never did well. It was the days of black and white television. Three networks. No cable, computers or cellphones. There was one particular show that Mom let me watch: *Laugh-In*. It was a very silly hour of goofy comedy. But, I emulated it. Nobody ever told me not to. I thought being liked meant that I was to be silly and goofy too. I had no reason to doubt it. Some people, even ones in my family, laughed at me, sometimes. I emulated nothing positive. Never someone who was good. Never someone who set a good example. It was like I lived in a foreign country and nobody understood anything I said. I followed no one because there was no one. I only saw goodness when I was with Mom-Mom and Pop-Pop. Otherwise, I forgot about it.

I hardly did anything, really. If there were cellphones, three-hundred cable television channels, a personal computer in my hand, and at my home, poof, it never happened. It was the lack of technology that allowed it. If there were surveillance cameras, UPC barcodes and the internet in the 1970s, it should've never happened. Everything I did was impossible in the twenty-first Century.

But, I did get away with it, and, at the same time, I got away with nothing. I had loose morals at the start of the decade, until I entered the navy toward the end of it. My wild ways followed me into the service, but I wasn't aware of the fact that I had no moral compass. Later I learned it didn't matter. I did nothing about it. I was to go through my childhood and youth morally blinded.

I was protected by *Mead*, and if I lived and wrote about these affairs without it, I would be writing from prison and I would've rotted and died there if *Mead* and the *m-team* didn't exist. These were magical interventions. But, I remained an automatic pilot…

Later in life, if a thought of doubt ever surfaced about *Mead* and its awesome power, I always recalled my very first day in the navy when another one of Mead's unbelievable interventions happened. I joined the navy…After the graduation ceremony, I just left the building. No friends. No plans. I just got in my car, and listened to music. I got high as I drove out to the racetrack. I lost, as usual. I always lost when I gambled, and I was never lucky at love. I believed I was an able body. I had to do something right. But it never happened because *Mead* planned otherwise. I blindly gave into all of my impulsivity. I always retained what I sang and played out what was in my heart. I tried, but I never succeeded…

I mentioned my love for cannabis. Bobby, a guy from school, who I was friendly with, had an older brother who sold it to me. He was also the one who fenced what I stole…

Mom bought me a suitcase as my graduation present. Her message: "Get the hell away from me." I moved from the east coast to the west coast, where Dad bought me a car in acknowledgment of my graduation.

Dad and Ellen did very well. They lived in Southern California. He became a real estate agent, and she was a magazine editor. I was a deadweight as soon as I arrived. Without a plan or even a goal what was I to do? I arrived full of emptiness; however, it was so profound this time. I took restaurant jobs because I was not prepared for adulthood. I looked back and I should have been eager to be a part of my father's real estate endeavors. I should've learned a lot. But I didn't. I was nothing. I was a loner. I had no social skills. I exceeded only in not exceeding. I was so troubled it led me to simply run away. I felt conflicted. If Dad wanted me to do something I always rejected it, but just in my mind. Once he wanted me to read a book about a baseball pitcher. I took the book. I thought that I even said thanks, but I never read it. I never even read the slip cover. I never knew why I refused to do what he wanted me to do. It's just that he wanted me to work, it didn't matter what I did. I wanted to do nothing. I smoked cigarettes every day. At night I smoked in the backyard of Dad's home. I listened to music and got high. I never thought about my future. I don't remember that I even thought about my plans for the next day.

In those days, it was unknown to me, but I had a mental illness, and it was to go untreated for a very long time… Before that, as I said, I ran away. I loaded up the car with my clothes, and I drove to Las Vegas, where I stayed for two-nights before I returned to California. *Mead* and the *m-team* worked tirelessly on me, and on my behalf. But, just like with Mom, I was a handful. If she ever knew how much of a handful I could have really been.

I recounted my thievery, but I left out something important. I had direct first hand knowledge and evidence that *Mead* and the *m-team* existed. The entity's vastness was unimaginable and incalculable to me. It observed me as a child, it watched me grow. But it wasn't until I became a teenager that *it* intervened. *Mead* and the *m-team's* interventions became so frequent that I never processed them in my mind. I never thought forward or backward in those days. I just responded to what I wanted at a particular time and moment, and I figured out how to get it. I was still a toddler.

Mead wanted me free. Every day and night I placed myself in a potential trap. Each day and night as *m-watchers* supervised, *m-workers* followed what was ordered. They rescued me. It was really something to see when I looked back at it. I played mindless games with *Mead*, until it all came to a head one night. There were so many times I should've been arrested. The number included all of my cannabis use. I never got caught with it. There were incidents when I should've been, but it never happened.

On one particular night in the spring the air was warm for that time of the year. Minutes earlier, on a whim, I drove from home to the bowling alley. It was the one across the street from where I grew up. I frequented it countless times as a kid. I returned that night to play the gambling machine. I played it often as a boy. I used change that I stole from my mother's purse, or that I found under Pop-Pop's recliner. .

Earlier that day, I followed through with a conspiracy to burglarize my place of employment of one particular drug. There were two five-hundred count bottles. It sat on a shelf where the pharmacist worked. Foolishly, I initially tried to steal it myself, but I was unsuccessful. The job required two other co-conspirators. So I revamped the plan to include them. One was Jennifer, a likable teenage blonde who worked at the store. It had a lunch counter, and she prepared food and waited on customers. The other person was Bobby. His brother arranged the transaction after it was all over. The plan unfolded like it was supposed to. Not even a hiccup of a mistake occurred. Later, I compensated my comrades. I fenced the stolen drugs the next day. Before that happened it sat in the trunk of my 1965 Ford, Galaxy 500. *Mead* watched everything.

As I drove to the bowling alley, I remembered that I reflected on my boyhood home. The place was a convenience that I never forgot. The home was situated on the corner of a relatively new neighborhood of identical row houses. Mine was adjacent to the strip mall; it was just across the street. We had a big, unfenced, yard beside the house with a giant weeping willow tree whose wistful sounds of swayed branches and rustled leaves could be heard with the window opened on a breeze filled summer's night.

I liked the old place. Mom moved us from our row home in the city to an apartment in Patriot Park. I was busy that summer; it's when I committed my first real crime. I was fifteen, and I spent the summer with Dad and Ellen in California.

I got a part time job. It was at night, and I worked alone. It always puzzled me why adults allowed me, at my age, to work alone at night. I was employed for less than a month. I quit the job after what happened. The store was robbed at knifepoint. I called the police and the owners to report it.

They arrived and I told them how it all happened. They bought it. I was never searched. I hid the money inside my bike's headlight just in case they did. Later, I casually rode my bike home; it never even fazed me. The next day, I quit. I told them my father told me that I wasn't allowed to work there anymore.

To highlight my idiocy it was that certain summer, through Ken, that I met another kid. I never remembered his name. He was fat and he wasn't cute. I was puzzled. I recalled the ride to the mall when we talked about friendship and cuteness. One kid said: "People only like you if you're cute," it was a sentence which blew me off course for decades. I had a hard time because I never understood.

I committed the crime on a whim. The idea came to mind. Immediately, without a thought, I did it, and I never lost any sleep. It was unknown to me why? I knew nothing about mental health (MH). I had never even heard the term before.

My trip to the bowling alley placed me on a city street. Trees lined one side, and a large old cemetery was on the other; it gave me no pause. There was a traffic light ahead. I got to the intersection and the green light turned yellow. I pressed the gas pedal a little and went through it. Within seconds I saw a police car in my mirrors; its lights flashed red like it warned me about my future.

Immediately, I pulled over. I kept very calm. I wondered, decades later, how? Not a hint of nervousness. I never crumbled. I never felt besieged. With hundreds of stolen prescription drugs in my trunk I should've. Two cops exited their vehicle and approached my car. Their flashlights beamed a strong bright light, which ricocheted off of the rear and side view mirrors.

Immediately, one of the officers used his flashlight to examine the backseat. The other told me that I was stopped because I ran through the light. I told him that I thought I had made it. He countered. He asked for my driver's license. I took out my wallet and I gave the piece of paper to him; it was not a plastic card with my picture on it in those days. The license was just a card made of special paper with my name, age, address, driver's license number, and the card's expiration date. I thought, years later, it should've been my expiration date.

Without a reason, the officer told me to get out of the car. I didn't ask questions. I just got out. I never freaked out. My angel face maintained its innocent ambiance all through the entire incident. I stood there as the officer dropped to his knees, and he shined his light under the car's front seat. Really, I never remembered that I had anything under it. But I did. The officer retrieved a small plastic bong; it was empty and dry. He rose to his feet and he looked at me for a second. I said: "That isn't mine. I don't know how it got there."

Anyone with an ounce of 21st Century common sense or watched any cop show knew, the policemen had probable cause to search the entire car at that point; it never happened. The officer confiscated the bong and he wrote me a ticket because I ran the light. I recalled that it was ten-dollars. Without a care in the world I got back inside the car, and it crossed my mind, if only they had looked in the trunk. I'd just be another convict who scribbled. I got back in the car and I drove to my destination, the bowling alley.

Mead and the *m-workers*, most likely, were outraged by all of my tomfoolery. Well, Bobby, the high school kid, who not only helped me with all of my marijuana and stolen property needs. He helped me and allowed me a privilege, and I enjoyed it immensely. I used my influence; it helped his older sister a great deal. I felt like *Don Corleone*.

After our graduation, Bobby and I went our separate ways. He helped me out, so I helped him when I got the chance. When I heard his sister's story of how she tried so very hard to get her SAG (Screen Actors Guild) card, but failed at every turn. Bobby said that she was so discouraged that she pondered what happened if she just came home. She lived in New York City and to get a SAG card it required that she obtain SAG employment; a *Catch-22*. So, all doors were closed to her. It was, until I learned of it. I had a cousin in New York City, and he directed television commercials. Through my aunt, I contacted him. He agreed to see Bobby's sister, and he hired her as an actress. Consequently, she got her SAG card. Bobby was more than pleased with me. So, when I contacted him before I was to go into the navy, I asked him to send me another ounce of marijuana. He did so with great ease. It was sent through *UPS*. The last time I saw Dad and Ellen was when I picked it up. I had no further contact with them until I left the navy, three years later, after I was honorably discharged.

I stood in formation in civilian clothes. I was that fresh to the scene. Within my first few minutes I was in trouble. Clueless, it was a good example of the kind of trouble *Mead*, I later learned, intervened. Immediately, I should've been arrested. I should've been charged, court martialled, and booted out of the Service. With that under my belt I would be sent to the brig, and a life of misery and despair. I stayed in a hotel at the navy's expense before I was transported to the Basic Training Reception Station. I was not blind, deaf or dumb; however, I acted so. I heard no opposition within me. And, I was as dumb as I ever was.

There were three RCDs. Each scorned us mercilessly. Their sharp eyes examined the nervous eyes of their new recruits. They stared at us up and down. It was at that point that I reached down and placed what was in my sock, a small marijuana pipe, and I put it in the zipper part of my gym bag, which was where I put the ounce that I brought along from Bobby. If it wasn't a sign that I was mindless then God help me. I actually brought an ounce of pot with me when I joined the navy. I acted like it was a toothbrush in my bag. I showed no reaction. I felt no fear.

Suddenly, another RDC came bursting out of the wooden building in front of us. He pointed to me and yelled: "Hey You." He ordered me and I followed him. He stopped, and he told me to take off my sneakers and socks. I followed his instructions. He saw nothing. He told me that he saw me put something into my sock. But after he found nothing he resigned himself.

Again, just like the police who pulled me over with five-hundred pills in my trunk, they had probable cause to go further and they didn't. Something stopped them. Something satisfied them. I realized decades later; it was *Mead*. Because if they took my small gym bag, emptied it and opened the zipper, again, my freedom ended right there. My life should've been altered. But they never searched. The suspicious drill sergeant sent me back into formation. Eventually, I was assigned a bed at the reception station barracks. When no one was around I took the ounce and hid it. I opened my new box of *Crest* toothpaste. I took the tube out and I put the ounce inside it. When I walked into the latrine, above the toilets there was a small opened air shaft. I stood on the toilet seat; it was a good fit. It was well hidden, I thought. I felt, suddenly, that it was unwise to take it with me to our Basic Training unit. I figured that it was not going anywhere, and would be okay, until I came back to get it.

I went through Basic Training just as foolishly as I always did with everything else. Halfway through the navy training, one night we got a pass. While some went to a movie on the base; others shopped for stuff at the PX, which is what I did. But then, I went back to those barracks at the reception station. It was full of brand new recruits. I remembered the sun had gone down and the lights in the billet were on. I was in uniform, a signal of status among new recruits. I walked in and said that somebody in my unit tricked me, that he hid my goddamn toothpaste in the air shaft. I went into the latrine, some followed, and I stood on the toilet seat and I retrieved it. I dropped it in my plastic shopping bag. I thanked the guys and left. Back at basic training, my toothpaste box lay in the bag as I opened it for inspection. Immediately, they were satisfied. I took it inside. I knew to place it somewhere. Later, I left the building and I walked around it. I found a small wooden door, which led to an area beneath the building. I opened the door and scooted in. I pulled the little door closed. The ground was layered in sand. I walked to a nearby corner and I buried the box in it. I emerged through the small door. I must have gone in and out of that area a handful of times over the eight weeks that I was there. Usually, I went under there after dinner, nobody ever saw me. Lucky?

The reason I got away with it was because one day, in the woods, I found a box turtle. I asked the RDC if we could make it our mascot; and he agreed. I took the turtle back to the building. I took complete charge of the entire project. I, and I alone walked the turtle, which meant I took it and I went beneath the building, smoked a little and returned with it. I made sure it had food and water, and upon my graduation from basic training the same RDC drove me to a wooded area where I released it.

I never feared anything. I never had any paranoia. However, I can say, without equivocation, something wasn't right. I smoked pot a thousand times. The pungent smell was on me, or it shouldn't have been. It should've been in the air of the rooms that I occupied. After I was permanently assigned a unit, I lived in the barracks. The odor should've made its way into the hallways from beneath the door of my room; it didn't. Health and welfare checks took place every month in the barracks. To get by this I decided the best place to hide my stash was in a baggy stuffed into my sock. I reasoned it was the last thing searched. I hid my pipe in a tissue box in the room. Again, no problems.

Once, I looked in the mirror and I saw my glassy eyes. I thought there were so many signals to my nefariousness. I never wondered back then, but I wondered many years later, why wasn't I caught? One word: *Mead*.

There was another side of me; it was my sexual stupidity. As I reported, my honesty and trustworthiness never developed properly. I never stole from individuals, only from businesses. I had this *Godfather* complex, everything I did, it was just business, and it made it okay. I also reported on my lack of any real friends because of the hyper-sexuality that I developed inadvertently as a kid. Tony entered my life. He had a huge home. It was the biggest and nicest I had ever been in. We played, but instead of ping-pong or billiards he sexualized me. I never understood until he did what he did. I had never been naked and had physical contact. He demeaned me. He commanded me to get on my knees and said: "suck me." I did what he said. It dawned on me when I thought of it years later, he was probably exposed to graphic pornography. It alerted the *m-team* who generated a pathway, which he embraced, and allowed him to do what he did. There were no VCRs or any technology used in the twenty-first Century, so he looked at pictures in a pornographic magazine.

I recognized, decades later, that I slowly withdrew from any dignity I may have had left inside of me towards myself. A process that slowly inched its way forward… The very first message that I remembered from *Mead* affected me the day it happened, and each and every day which followed. It came about during the Holy religious days of the Jewish New Year. As their offspring, Mom stemmed from the highly religious arm of the Jewish faith. While Dad stemmed from the same religion but his family were not religious. On Mom's side: Mom-Mom and Pop-Pop were religious; they were members of, and frequently attended an Orthodox Synagogue. They also kept kosher, and they didn't work on Saturdays. On Dad's side: Annie and Harry were not observant. They never kept kosher, Mom said that they ate spareribs at their favorite Chinese restaurant every Saturday for lunch. Mom-Mom and Pop-Pop were self-employed, they sold shoes at swap meets/flea markets. Annie sold jeans at a swap meet, I heard, the origins of which were dubious.

Annie and Harry moved to Hollywood, California in the mid 1960s, so I only had minimal contact with them as a child. The first time I visited them was because Dad and Ellen put me on a bus from Missouri to Los Angeles; it took days. So, Mom sent me to Dad for the summer and Dad sent me to Annie and Harry. I visited them, once, in the summer. I got to go to *Disneyland by* myself. One day, when I visited, Harry sat on his favorite chair and puffed away on his pipe. I stood in front of him. I was filled with glee as he pulled out his money clip and he gave me twenty-dollars to go. I took city buses, both ways. It is now impossible for me to imagine myself taking buses, at age eleven from Hollywood, in Los Angeles County, to *Disneyland* in Orange county, where the park was located, but I did. I returned to the east and settled in for the coming year. At the end of summer, it was always religious time.

I walked from the Orthodox Temple to the Reformed Temple. I decided to sit on the balcony. I searched for my religion at different times in my life, and on that day, I found some. There wasn't a soul on the balcony. The service was in session. I went to the front row, sat down, and picked up a copy of the Old Testament. I opened it and I looked down. The words popped off the page: *Thou shall not lay with a man the way thou lays with a woman.* I quickly closed the book, stood up and walked out.

It was *Mead's* first attempt to straighten me out but it never did. I hobbled my way through high school. I hung out with others, but I had no real friends. My sexual drive led to a lot of masturbation because I had no physical contact with anyone my age. There was an adult woman in her late 20s, who propositioned me and we had sex four times.

But the real intervention happened when I served in the navy. I was raped twice, by the same man within a three-week period. We weren't at sea; it happened on base. The first time he lured me into the supply room, which was where he worked. He was a petty-officer who I had never met or seen before. I was a seaman recruit. The guy was big and strong. It was the first time I ever took it. It was not done on a voluntary basis. Three weeks later, he did it again. He saw me after work. I never saw him. He followed me into my barracks; it was worse than the first. The next day, I met with the Lieutenant Commander and I told him, emotionally, I wanted to move from my barracks. I never told him about what happened; I still worked at my unit, but, as far as where I lived, I was moved into a totally different location that day. I never saw the guy again. Not at the chow hall. Not at the movie theater. Not at the PX. Not anywhere on base.

I was blinded by *Mead*. I was raped twice but I never reported it because I had an attraction to my own gender, and back then, if the navy knew, I would be discharged dishonorably, with haste. They were items that were folded and put away in a file in a drawer that *Mead* and the *m-workers* created and controlled. They brought it out and used it later for punishment.

It was the very beginning of it all. The *m-workers* blinded me and erased the impact and trauma of the rapes; not the memory because I knew what had happened. Rather, it was what I thought and felt. I never thought about it. I felt nothing. I was numb to it all. I lived as if it was nothing, and I acted as if it all never occurred. PTSD constantly hounded me decades later along with another tool of *Mead* and the *m-team*; the cluster headache.

It was the worst pain imaginable, and it went on for decades. These were the kinds of daily traumas that made life unbearable. They, the cluster headaches, acted differently on me. I never felt the sensation of guilt. I was aware of my actions because they were all locked away in storage, but that was it. The trauma of the rapes. The crimes that I carried out. All were kept tightly sealed inside me. *Mead* never erased traumas. *M-workers* placed them on hold. They were revealed, eventually, for me to ponder, and cope with. I went on with my life.

I returned to the States because *Mead* intervened again. I was threatened; someone wanted to defame me for my homosexuality because I didn't help his friend. He needed me to lie and cheat. The next day, out of the blue, I got word that Pop-Pop was dying, and the Red Cross made arrangements for me to receive an early discharge, since my real discharge date was just three-months away. I left that afternoon, and flew back, was processed through and given my DD214, proof of my military service.

As Mom drove me to see Mom-Mom and Pop-Pop the gurney with Pop-Pop's body had just exited the apartment. Mom screamed and fell to her knees. We went inside and there was Mom-Mom being consoled by Lily.

Mead saved me, and taught me lessons. But at the same time, I started the very long process of shutting myself down.

I entered the very best period of my life, which was soon followed by the very worst.

Chapter 7

Lily went to college with a huge political appetite. She majored in political science, and her education was covered by Uncle Stu, who had wealth.

She was a serious person with a soft heart. She kept yesterday's headlines alive. She was a political activist on issues like guns and abortion. She also offered her opinions on what she called the State of the World. Lily told us, if she had the power, every country in the world would lay down all weapons and create a World Choir. Each country trained, Lily explained to me, armies of baritones and sopranos. They would compete with nations who they had an adversarial relationship with. The winner, selected by AI, ended with the words that it "made the world a better place."

Before I entered the navy, Lily called me and invited me to a concert; it was a group we both listened to. She thought of others quite a lot. I was not on her top ten list, however, because I was too busy with my criminality.

Her brown hair casually rested on her shoulders when she met me at the train depot. I was not prepared for the invitation. I was surprised by it, actually. She lived in a small brick apartment dwelling. She had a first-floor studio apartment in what she told me was: "the gay section of town." She wasn't gay so I wondered why she moved to this location. I looked around the room. Off to one corner was a small kitchenette. An inexpensive gray futon sat behind a small half barrel coffee table. She had plants and flowers hung by her window; a poster of Albert Einstein, and books. Lily loved books. She had many. Her addiction was healthy, I thought. She didn't read constantly, but when she had free time, I always caught her eyes in a book when we were younger. She loved both fiction and non-fiction. Her favorite author was John Steinbeck and her favorite book of his was *The Pearl*. Her favorite movie was *The Treasure of the Sierra Madre*. The raw truth of humanity. We all had a good side and a bad side, I thought.

Chapter 8

Glenda quickly climbed the ladder of *PROX NEWS*. There she reached the pinnacle of her career. It was the number-one prime-time show on cable, yet alone cable news. She had a twenty-million dollar contract, a one-hundred thousand dollars for wardrobe, a one-million dollar expense account, and a chauffeured limousine that carried her to and from the studio. She had a penthouse in Manhattan, and a home just outside the city.

She interviewed Pliartrumn at one of his eight-therapeutic retreats. Retreat members paid a two-hundred-thousand-dollar initiation fee to join his club at Matuffa. The way he put it: "There are two-ballrooms. In each five-star luxury suite the bathroom has a chandelier, a dust free chandelier, can you believe it? It has a marble floor, and many other attractions people will thoroughly enjoy. The best meat. The best seafood. The best wine and the best massage spas in the entire world; the entire world. Can you believe it? You can't find anything better, anywhere. It's the greatest spa in the history of spas, and folks, there's a long rich history there; a real long history; I can tell you that. My spas are more popular than the Roman baths were in Julius Caesar's day. People traveled from all over the world just to spend their time at a Pliartrum Retreats. We have the world's most fantastic therapeutic services. Did I say that? In the State of Oregon, we broke ground on our new psilocybin retreat; what a place it'll be. I guarantee you'll love it…"

Each of his retreats had an impressive facade with an entrance typical of the lavish Pliartrum brand. He sold everything from Pliartrum saline nasal spray to Pliartrum's moisturizer for dry skin. There was Pliartrum ointment for toe-fungus. Pliartrum gel for shaving. A remedy for hemorrhoids. Pliartrum's aspirin, cough drops, prophylactics, morning after pill, antacid, witch-hazel and epsom-salt.

Many of his therapeutic retreats were just for show; most of them lost money. He made his real money from the drugs his company created, developed and distributed. Better put his ties to organized crime because that's what it was. He was a player way back when. He peddled addictive drugs to Americans. Then came a pandemic which had been predicted by many and ignored by many more.. There were many deaths; it chiefly targeted those from his own political constituency. Its consequences led to the deaths of nearly one-hundred thousand people in just one year of his presidency. The king of Big Pharma and his empire of retreats, health centers and pain clinics all bore his name, predominantly. At night, the familiar letters were illuminated all over the country.

I thought of my sister, awash in her power and material wealth, and I suddenly realized that *PROX-NEWS-NETWORK;* should've been called PROXY-NEWS-NETWORK because they were just a proxy; a mouthpiece for the Country Club Party. Or, better yet, *MNN, Mead's News* Network, primarily because of the *m-team* of Mead's western hemisphere division. That division, as well as the eastern one, were guided by the *Executives*, who took their inspiration from God. They turned inspiration into reality. There were pockets of peace and tranquility, which stemmed from the first millennia. There was always conflict between humans. It was to test them. Be it at a barber shop or a beauty parlor. A bank or a beach. A breakfast brunch or part of the mob who stormed the U.S. Capitol after President

Pliartrum lost his bid for re-election. Conflict was as plentiful as water. Be it through family, neighbors and friends. On street corners, at the end of a cul-de-sac, on roads, on bridges or highways. In the family. Spouses, siblings, and the unit as a whole suffered. In addition, there was conflict between races, ethnic groups, religions, genders and sexual identities. People had the ability to work through any conflicts in a healthy, positive, productive environment. Be it the boss, or a conflict with a supervisor, a co-worker or a customer.

Conflict was everywhere, just like it's always been ever since the dawn of man. And it continued until the day came when the people learned the lesson that conflict killed. People decided no more, and they lived in peace. But some never wanted peace. When born each person had a level of savagery in them. Some were microscopic; it barely registered in the data. Others alternated between the two every day. But there were some who constantly engaged in it. They had it in their minds, hearts and deeds. Their desire was to hurt someone, mentally or physically, and to gain pleasure from it. People who had zero empathy for their fellow beings. In fact, they gained great satisfaction as they watched the humans they've hurt, suffer. It's their goal, to reap power and energy through hatred, cruelty and tyranny, and to watch humans suffer; it was a national pastime to them. They were lost in evil, and they got their power from it. The good side gets their power and influence through goodness; it's much more pleasant, and it's a lot less messy.

The stage was set. The Country Club Party members were under the complete control of *Mead* and the *m-team* because it was that time in human history, once again. Mead had pitted brother against brother; the deadliest of all conflicts. In the nineteenth-century there was America's Civil War; it accounted for six-hundred-twenty-thousand deaths. World War II was considered the deadliest conflict in all of history. In the twentieth-century World War I and World War II created over seventy-million deaths combined. So with twenty-first century technology and arsenals, those numbers for the brother-against-brother war, which when added to another World War, meant the number exceeded the twentieth-century's by a mile.

M-*workers* worked in the trenches; *it* drove all conflict, and *it* instantaneously generated important data which was channeled back to the m-watchers, which was shared with the *m-team*: Who cheated on their spouse. Who struck a young child across the face because he said something. Who masturbated out of loneliness. Who instigated? Who peed their bed as a child. Who worked and played in harmony. Who created friction and ill will at home, work, school and at play. Data was sent and received every second. Some actions were rendered instantaneously; impulsivity was a very strong tool of *Mead's*; the human's propensity to do the wrong thing. To make the wrong choice. Until the day when a lesson was finally learned. The individual made the final decision. It was up to them whether to do good or bad. Whether to make the correct common sense moral choice or the wrong one. These decisions ran the gambit. People who were forced onto a path, wondered how and why they got to where they were. Sometimes, it led to catastrophe in their lives which included death. But, occasionally, it led to a better world. *Mead* worked in mysterious ways. Simple things: What I should've worn that day? Easy things: what I should've eaten for lunch? Tough things: I should've helped my out-of-work mentally ill brother with money? Even tougher things: I should've married or I should've divorced? Hard things: I should not have taken that drink? Harder things: I should not have drank the whole bottle. Finally, bad things: I should've hurt her. I should've killed his dog. And, then the just plain evil things: I should've murdered them. I should've shot up a school, my workplace, a Synagogue or a church, a grocery store or a nightclub.

If there were blue skies, Glenda insisted to her viewers there was something wrong. The other political party, aside from the Country Club Party, knew nothing. They were cowards, according to her, and heathens. They wanted to sexualize children. They were evil. It was meant for people who demoralized and dehumanized because only they knew the truth, which was always exactly what Pliartrum wanted. The sky wasn't blue to them or to their viewers. *Mead* and the *m-team* stayed on task. *Mead* blinded Glenda and her network, which blinded their viewership. It shielded them from the other political party. Glenda claimed that they were corrupted people. That they never told the truth. They created, instigated and pursued conflict; it was their daily duty. Glenda's news network, however, distorted the truth. They distracted their audience from reality. She explained that they saved their viewership from a world filled with audacious humans who destroyed society. Nighty, they filled their audience with the kind of information that humans of the twentieth-century found on *Green Acres*. Glenda targeted nearly one-half of the U.S. population with her nightly diatribes on how great a man Pliartrum was, and how awful, crazed and disgusted his political opponents were. She lied over and over. I was sickened by it. I watched Glenda most of the time just to see what she was up to, and then I turned on another news network for the truth.

Chapter 9

Lily and Manuel lived in the middle of nowhere. The spacious single story dwelling was spread out. Behind it was a sizable lake. Lily sold her pottery business for a handsome sum of money; she became a third-grade teacher at a local elementary school. Manuel attended the same school. The boy in the fifth-grade had mood swings. He stole; he was deceitful and he lied. According to one of his friends, Manuel was well liked. Lily said that she talked to another mother whose kid said that Manuel had a hot temper.

He was not happy at times. He manipulated other kids. They thought that he had more power because his Mom was a teacher at the school. He ordered them around like he was king of the school. He played with other kids but he never respected them or their property. If a kid was nice to him he'd be a really nice guy. On one particular day, Manuel stole a boy's lunch money. The accuser insisted that Manuel took it out of his desk when he and the other kids went to the boy's room. Manuel denied it, but the vice-principal vetoed; she accepted none of it; she got wind of Manuel's temper and deceitfulness; Lily had talked to her about it. She searched him, and she found the money; it was exactly to the penny to what the other boy had reported.

The vice-principal interrupted Lily's class to tell her. She listened as the school's second in command whispered into her ear: Her eyes widened; Manuel was non-compliant. He refused to let her paddle him because he stole some money. Lily's face turned sour. The kids in her class saw her roll her eyes. Most kids hushed up. One kid laughed. Lily motioned for the class assistant to take over. As the heavy-set middle aged woman rose and slowly moved to the front of the room. Lily and the vice-principal exited. Manuel's mother looked worried.

He was paddled that day. Lily gave consent, but she told me that her heart sank when it happened. The boy took the punishment.

It seemed to me that they never ever really healed from that day. Manuel became worse as he aged.. He had temper tantrums before, but they were nothing like when he hit his teens. He had trouble with law. He burglarized a neighbor's home and he took cash off a table. The police were contacted; they determined that Manuel was the culprit. He talked his way out of it. But when Lily learned of it she suspected him right away. He had forty-dollars on him when they went out to dinner the same night, I was told. They had stopped at a *Walmart*, and she was surprised because the next thing she knew he bought a video game. She asked him where he got the money. He told me that the money and the video game belonged to another kid, and that he was given the money, and he was told to buy it for this other kid. Lily asked him who? He told her I can't tell you because he'd get into trouble. He was no longer a suspect in her mind; she knew that he was the thief. Lily was soft. In her delicate female way she asked Manuel about it. He said that she berated him. That she picked apart every move he made. She never called the police, but she should've. And she should've told the neighbor the truth but she never did. She never explained why she let Manuel get away with it. Then I thought of *Mead*, and I saw things much clearer. Lily was blinded by *it* on that particular day…

When Manuel reached the age of fifteen, Lily put all of the pieces of the puzzle together. Angelica did some research. Apparently, she got her hands on a report. It said that Manuel was given up from adoption. Also, it reported that he was in and out of three different foster homes before the age of four. He was at Child Protective Services for two-weeks before Angelica's agency was contacted again. They never helped CPS when they tried to place the boy before, they knew about him, a flier was circulated, but at the time they had no vacancies. It was the next day, however, when Angelica talked with Lily about him. I never hesitated for a second, she told me. She went to meet the boy. That's all it took. She was hooked. She told me later that she thought that he knew how to charm and manipulate someone even back at that age.

The file on Manuel revealed that he was the product of teenage "hanky-panky." His mother was a naive young woman; she never knew that she was even pregnant until her water broke. The father was a sixteen-year-old. His name was revealed but CPS never went after him. He was categorized as Latino, which followed a DNA match.

His light brown skin was quite a contrast to Lily, who, literally, was lily-white. Look at the walls of their home and it seemed that Lily and Manuel were a very happy mother and son. They went everywhere, and they did everything together. The framed photos captured the pair at *Disneyland*, *Six Flags Magic Mountain*, cruises, the beach, the mountains, and Washington, D.C.. Lily loved this country, and so as part of the child's introduction into American society, they spent four-nights in the city. They toured the White House, the Capitol, the Washington Monument, the Lincoln Memorial, the Zoo, and many of the museums.

As I reflected, I recognized that Manuel's real problem was, consequently, a dangerous one, and it brewed in him like a coffee. There were little indicators along the way; however, it became very apparent when he reached his mid-teens. They always had their arguments as he grew up, but then they both made up with one another. After that everything was good for a while.

Chapter 10

Frank once referred to Boris, who was now a teen, as a wanna-be philosopher because the boy wrote down and offered his thoughts on things like the covid pandemic. The respiratory infectious disease killed many people across the globe; it hit the U.S. hard too, thanks to President Rich Pliartrum. Frank said there was a run on toilet paper at Walmart. Boris, Frank reported, laughed and said it was due to the fact that everyone was full of shit. This youngin had an unusual approach to life; he constantly berated others. A "smart-ass punk" as Frank once uttered.

The boy's attitude befuddled me. He was the kind of kid when encountered, by an adult, they'd loved to forget they ever laid eyes on him. It wasn't always that way. As a young child he, and his Mom and Dad were all very happy. After Sarah was born, Boris changed… The adolescent became so idiotic, obnoxious and bittersweet. Mom-Mom said that Boris had a chip on his shoulder as big as a log. From his mother and father to the mailman. From his teacher in school to the bus driver. To him, every single one of us sucked. Adults welcomed his departure. Back then he walked around with a permanent scowl on his face. I recalled that on his last birthday, Glenda sent him a card with fifty-dollars. He looked at it and said: "I love that woman." His reality was warped. Deep down, in a deep dark catacomb of his mind was the real person. The rational mind. The senses of the mind which found pleasure in the smell of a flower or the sight of beautiful painting. It was quite the opposite. Boris had one hobby; violent video games, which Frank allowed. But, the father of the brat was out maneuvered. Boris pushed his buttons repeatedly. One time, Boris yelled at Frank: "You're no fucking good, and so if everybody else in this goddamn world." Frank lost it and he smacked the boy across the face, which sent him flying across a coffee table, and in the process he cracked a rib. CPS got involved. Nothing happened, but Frank walked more tenderly around Boris after that.

Frank comforted his daughter, who was, understandably, afraid of her brother. Frank told her that he was brainwashed by the People Party. Sarah never understood, and, frankly, I never thought about my niece much. When I saw the skinny young girl with blonde hair, which was genetically handed down through Pat's family. She looked shy and reserved. She never sought attention. She had perfect social skills, which she also received from her Mom. Frank, filled the little girl's head with all of Glenda's and Pliartrum's talking points. The small young lady sat, patiently, and listened to him go on and on.

Boris was diagnosed with *Antisocial Personality Disorder, ASPD*, when he was fifteen. He was in and out of behavioral programs and institutions, one after another but it was too late… The boy's behavior in the home angered Frank a great deal. He told me about the time when he sat across from a MH worker at one of the behavior programs he was in. The experience, he recalled, reminded him of the time when he gave up a vicious family pet. It was euthanized at the animal shelter.

Things used to be a lot normal. The father went to work everyday as the mother tended the house. As Boris grew Frank became his Little League coach. Boris was a pitcher. Frank heaped praise upon him. "The kid," Frank said, "was a great pitcher." A decade or more passed and the boy did not become Sandy Kofax. Frank's interests changed. He mostly ignored Boris and Pat, as the 2016 Presidential election heated up. He loved one guy, Pliartrum. "He says it like it is. He's not some fucking politician. I like the guy." He may have started a love affair with candidate Pliartrum, but he was not spared from the angst that Boris generated. The kid was every parent's nightmare. What every parent dreaded. That they had conceived and brought into this world, a monster. Someone who horrified and terrorized the community. In the twenty-first century, it wasn't just the community who was affected. Mass media reported the truly horrifying news; and it spread like a wildfire across the country.

Boris' problems started in the family. It included genetics, environment, traumatic experiences and upbringing. He was exposed to adult violence, horror and sex, and he handled it extremely poorly. After the boy pestered him, Frank said it was okay if he watched *The Texas Chainsaw Massacre*. It stimulated all the wrong senses in him; his psychosis, which switched on like a light when he sensed there was prey. He learned he gained satisfaction when he watched or participated in something where people suffered; he got off on it.

Before his early institutionalization, it was one explosion after another. *M-workers* were busy after *m-watchers* witnessed an aggression by Boris, after he punched Sarah in the face. The data showed that he gained pleasure from the memory. He played it over and over again in his mind because it made him feel "powerful. He smeared his feces on a gift that Pat gave to her for her birthday. And he outright bullied everyone on a regular basis. It got to the point that Frank placed a padlock on his bedroom door. He sent him to his room often and locked him in; the boy was locked up if there was an incident. Or when he was not supervised; especially at night. Frank was beside himself; he was only comforted by Pliartrum and his 2016 Presidential campaign. That's all he talked about. He socialized with his gentile friends. He never had any Jewish friends when he was young because Mom moved us out to Patriot Park, so Frank never got to go to the JCC like I did. All of my socialization was with other Jewish kids. "He made friends with Goys," Mom once said.

He wanted to put Boris into another program. If they waited he risked their place on the waiting list, especially for teenagers. It seemed the twentieth-century's juvenile delinquents, those of yesteryear, were tamed in comparison to the SMI (seriously mentally ill) teens of the twenty-first century. A healthy chunk of them were like Boris. He liked knives. In particular, his hunting knife. It was a birthday gift from his Aunt Glenda. She knew that Frank and Boris camped out. It was before he became a teenager. Boris was one of those volatile kids who was bombarded with technology. Violent video-games, graphic television and graphic violence on the internet led them to be at the worst. He courted evil. There were ramifications to a set of immature eyes. A child can't process what they saw. What was meant only for mature adults. The images and behaviors disturbed his young psyche. It exposed him. It seemed that the disturbed youngster set the stage for tragedy. *Mead* along with the *m-team* and the *m-workers* ensured most children were spared from exposure to adult violence, sex and pornography; it waited until they handled it on a mature level. Severely disturbed young people slipped through the cracks. or, once again, it was meant to be... They were exposed and it damaged their minds. Boris was one of those kids.

After Boris punched Sarah in the face it led to juvenile court, which cost Frank more money. The judge decided the boy must be counseled. He stated that the youngster had been through enough behavioral programs. Frank spent hundreds of dollars for his so-called counseling; it lasted six-months.

Boris was a very sick young man. Frank never stopped his son from his exposure to adult excesses; sex, violence and pornography. "Why," I asked him once? He threw up his hands, and said: "There's no stopping him." The student of evil accessed and researched everything he shouldn't; made possible by twenty-first century technology. The fact was that he lived on the edge of psychosis. He teetered back and forth ever since he was twelve. But he wasn't diagnosed until he was thirteen. It all contributed to what he did. It made him worse. He was, I believed, left to fester. Only, the infection got worse.

Boris sat upon the video game chair he got for Christmas from Frank and Pat. The boy's trigger fingers got a lot of exercise as he played. He had no friends. He never had a healthy normal relationship. He never dated. He never socialized with anyone. When he attended public school he had no extracurricular activities. He dropped out of high school in the tenth-grade. Pat fought him, practically, everyday. But he refused to go to school. People distracted him. I remembered Frank once said that his offspring had no connections to anyone except for those who played video games with him online.

The saddest expiration dates were those of the beloved who were of great age; if murder was added into the equation; it produced a shock to a person's central nervous system.

Found only after she missed church, a ninety-year old woman was savagely murdered in her home. It happened on a quiet residential street in Patriot Park, an area not prone to the kind of savagery the detectives, on scene, found. Detective J.D. Wicks worked for the city. The word came down to him on a day of rest. It was anything but. He emerged from the victim's home after he looked at everything under a microscope inside. He inspected his people's work in the garden beds. He saw his fingerprint woman in action, as she dusted the window sills. He inspected a shed, and as came out, a flock of ducks honked, as they flew by overhead. He watched them. He admired ducks, and his grimace face mellowed for a second, that is, until he noticed a home nested above the victim's, 100-yards away. Suddenly, he had a hunch. He walked back inside the house, into the kitchen, and looked out its window above the murderer victim's sink. The football field distance intrigued him for some reason. His *M-watchers* ordered *m-workers* to action. *They* steered him, all of the sudden, to that window many yards away.

Through the kitchen window Pat saw the police activity in the distance. Yellow tape surrounded the murder house.

Officers, some who wore protective gear, others who were uniformed, came in and out carrying brown paper bags, which they held in their rubber-gloved hands. Officials entered, solemnly, and exited disturbed; as if they witnessed something that would haunt them for the rest of their lives, according to the lead detective.

Pat said, later, that she always gazed out the window while she rinsed or washed things; she liked doing it. Frank's backyard, with the built-in swimming pool, which he prized, was completely fenced. On the other side of it, Pat had a view that she had seen all of her life, a wooded area filled with trees that shed their leaves every year. She later told me that she had looked over the trees, and down at one particular house, "Ever since I was tall enough," she said. In the winter, when the tree branches were bare, she had an even better view. At the kitchen window of the two homes, Pat said that she watched a family who grew up there. She remembered that she saw kids, a grown-up man and woman at their kitchen window ever since she remembered. They each had a bright light above the sink. Pat looked down at the house and its residential street. "I watched a family change." When she thought about it, she said that ten-years ago, she noticed the man and the woman still appeared in the window. That was it. Years passed, and then there was only the woman. She never saw the man anymore. "Just her," Pat said. She never knew who the old woman was who appeared at the kitchen sink. But everybody in Frank's house, especially Pat's Mom and Dad, knew of the old woman, who, by now, was old, gray and hunched over. She still washed her dishes, Pat recollected.

As Pat rinsed a coffee cup she listened to a reporter, live, on the television, who was at the scene of the brutal murder. She turned off the water because her eyes couldn't believe what her ears heard. Between the reporter's voice and the sight she witnessed over the trees, down at the old woman's house, she cringed. There were emergency and police vehicles with the red-lights flashing. She saw two men at the kitchen window. She later learned that they were detectives. When Frank came home that day from work, he was surprised; his wife was drinking. She usually waited until after dinner, when she would go to the Legion that she worked at on weekends, and on her days off, she went there too. She drank, smoked and socialized there seven-days a week. Frank said that she had a glass of vodka mixed with orange-juice in her hand that day. She was seated on the sofa, glued to the television. They talked about the old woman and her murder. Pat told him what she saw out the kitchen window. Suddenly, the reporter's voice caught their attention. She reported that the victim's name was Betty Laslo, and that she was ninety-years old.

Frank sighed, after he stood and looked back at his wife. He was so sick of how much Pat drank and smoked; he never smoked cigarettes. It was bad enough that he made her sleep on the sofa, because she reeked too much to lay with, he said. Pat told me that Frank didn't love her anymore. "Her drinking was such that she hid bottles around the house," he said. She told me, later, it was the day she knew that Frank didn't love her anymore. Once, she told me, with emotion, that Frank brought her home from the hospital. Her hospitalization was related to her health problems for her addictions to alcohol and pain-pills peddled by Pliartrum. She had an accident. She bled through her tampon onto the car seat that she sat on. She cried when she said that "Frank wouldn't help me. He left me there in a pool of blood."

Sarah came through the screen-door and saw the look on her parent's faces. "What's the matter," she asked as she kissed Pat on the cheek. Frank looked worried; his thoughts were elsewhere. "If he had any hair on his head his hands would've been through it by now," Pat told me.

Frank sat back down on the sofa. Sarah watched the news and her parent's reactions. Pat told Frank that she watched several uniformed police officers outside the home. She imagined, she told him and me, that inside it, there were plain clothed detectives who carefully examined the scene of the crime. The sight of sin sat on the sofa, Wicks would tell her later. Pat said to me, on the phone, that the elder had a gaping wound on her neck. "A vicious attack." Pat's brow sank suddenly, she had a thought that she wanted to write down. She opened the drawer of an old wooden coffee table in front of the sofa. In it she found a pen, and she also found a school paper, which belonged to Boris. She twinged after she opened it. She saw that he got an "F," but, much worse, was what she read:

"Don't ever laugh when a hearse goes by or you may be the next to die. They wrap you up in a bloody sheet and send you down six-million feet. The worms go in and the words go out. They eat your intestines and spit them out. Your eyes pop out, your teeth decay and that's the end of a happy day."

Frank read the note as the screen door opened, Frank's and Pat's eyes focused on Boris. Sarah focused on her parents who looked like they'd seen a ghost. Boris smirked and asked: "What the hell's wrong with you?" Pat and Frank looked at each other for a second. Frank said that he asked him what he did that day. He replied, according to my brother, that he "did nothing."

"Weren't you at school?" He looked at Pat, who said: "Oh, I told him this morning that he didn't have to go if he didn't want to."

Frank communicated: "Well, if you weren't in school then where were you?" Silence filled the room as if nobody was in it.

"Why the questions," Boris asked? "What do you mean bombarding me with - where you been! I don't have to tell you where I've been." "I'd like to hear what other activities you had today, that's all," Frank recounted on the witness stand.

"Why?"

"No reason, son. Just checking on your well-being, that's all."

"When did you ever give a fuck about me well being," he shot back.

"I should take off my leather belt"

. "Well go ahead, Frank, take it off."

"Boris, did you know that the old lady was killed, Pat interjected?"

"What old lady," he quipped.

Pat looked at Frank for his reaction. Her eyes, immediately, shifted to Boris, and she said: "You know, the old lady we see out the kitchen window, sometimes."

"I don't know who you're talking about," he uttered, and went down the hall, into his room and closed the door. Sarah looked frightened. Her dad, she told me, comforted her, that everything would be okay. Both adults rose and walked into the kitchen. The agreement they came to took less than ten-seconds. Frank opened a kitchen door and pulled out the padlock that he used to put on Boris' bedroom door. Pat picked up the phone. Sarah walked in the room; she watched her parents uneasiness. When she saw the padlock in Frank's hand, she stopped him, and asked in a worried manner: "Can I stay overnight at Peggy's house?" Frank nodded and began to walk down the hallway to Boris' room.

Pulsates of recall energy were generated by the *m-workers*. The order went out from the *m-watchers*: deep data was to be collected.

Chapter 11

I filled a pot full of water and placed it on the stove to make Ramen Noodles. I was vividly reminded of Lily's notebook, and how her writing seemed to boil over. She thought that Pliartrum politics was madness.

I knew it was *Mead*.

Orders came down from the *Executives*, who in consultation agreed the turmoil was necessary; maybe this time people laid down their weapons and helped and tolerated each other. God signed off on the pivotal but routine action, which was created, once again, to test mankind who had failed miserably time and time again.

 Pliartrum was always a player in the crimes of big-pharma. He became the leader of it when he took office as President. His crimes took place before, during and after he was in office. Crimes against the country and humanity. My water boiled. With the election of President Pliartrum, the Country-Club Party believed that they controlled demonic entities from Organized Crime to the Nazis; not, however, when their leaders were in sync with them. The old and established party was blinded by *Mead;* it challenged the sanctity of the core value of this nation; its democracy. However imperfect it was.

The boiled water overflowed the pot. While the Nazi-fide Pliartrum groups trashed the capital, and the country-club political party with it. I turned off the burner, but the water kept on boiling. They wanted their party back, but they feared the monster they created. They knew it ate country-club party members for Sunday brunch. The water was still hot; its steam rose and hovered over the pot like a dark cloud.It needed to be cooled off but it was easier said than done; it was as hot as hell in the kitchen and I needed to leave before I melted like the Wicked Witch of the West in *The Wizard of Oz*.

The m-workers gathered data which suggested certain circumstances of three humans intersected and it required the lightning attention of *m-planners*. Lily watched a Youtube video on Pliartrum's disposition with the law. It was late on a Saturday night. The west coast wrapped up its day in an hour, but it was already early morning on the east coast. On very rare occasions the *m-team* and *m-workers* used their magic and performed a rare intervention. A power that literally took over the person's little-voice in their head. The one we trust. The one who warns or encourages. The little voice tallied the data: What a person thought and felt. The *m-team* then ordered the *m-workers* into action. Was it good? Did it spread goodness, kindness, and tolerance? Or was it bad. Only conflict that spreads violence and intolerance like soft butter on a slice of crispy toast.

Because on that night the stars aligned so closely it required all hands on deck for the *m-team*.

The *m-team* summoned the leader of each *m-worker* who oversaw these certain individuals: Glenda, Lily and former President Pliartrum. The connection between Glenda and the washed-up leader of the free world was well established. He appeared on her show regularly. Sometimes it was two or three times a week; it depended on the news. But, to him, it was never enough. He wanted the Pliartrum name on the tip of each American's tongue. Good or bad. He just loved being on top, the person everyone talked about everyday, all the time, morning, noon and night. Whether good or bad, he accepted all of the publicity he could get. He wanted good press, of course. But, he knew bad press happened as well.

The video was four-minutes long. It appeared on one of Youtube's regular political pundit's channels. The suggestion from the commentator was that Pliartrum was immune from being imprisoned for his crimes against the American people. Lily told me that she watched it and worked on her comment before she posted it late that Saturday night. It read: *If we need to build one just for them, Pliartrum, his family, and all of his co-conspirators must be prosecuted and imprisoned. The greatest traitors that this country has ever seen, can't go unpunished. Pliartrum's Prison can be built on the hundreds-of-thousand acres of federal land in the Nevada desert. He can slap his name on it just like his other ill-gotten retreats, and clinics. Illegitimate because they were all built on the backs of hundreds of thousands of victims of his drugs. People he just stepped on in his quest for power, but he and the others MUST face serious consequences. His secret service details can work in shifts guarding his prison cell. As to* C-Country Club Party members *who* just stood *by to shove these lies down the throats of the American people. You should all be incarcerated in Pliartrum too! Don't let organized crime rule America! Stop them before it's too late!*

Lily called me about nine that next morning. I sensed from her alert tone something unusual had happened. It appeared to her that Pliartrum responded to the Youtube comment that she wrote late last night. This morning he posted this on his social media platform:

No President has done more for Israel than I have. Somewhat surprisingly, however, our wonderful Christian Right friends are far more appreciative of this than the people of the Jewish faith, *especially those living in the U.S. Those living in Israel, though, are a different story- Highest approval rating in the World, could easily be P.M.! The U.S. Jews* have to get their act together and appreciate what they have in Israel - Before it is too late!

She argued it was the timing and the words made it clear to her that he responded to what she wrote the previous night. Hers was posted late that night. Pliartrum's post appeared early the next morning. She also pointed to how he ended his post, which, again, she attributed to her comment on the Youtube video. She said it blew her mind that the former president's people read posts to videos and shared them with him under certain circumstances. Apparently, Lily met those circumstances. Also, of course, her name appeared above her comment; it was easy to deduce from her last name her heritage.

We talked for an hour. Lily believed Pliartrum became irate over certain sentences and specific words that she put into her comment. He responded the way he did, the former President of the United States, the most powerful person in the World, because he lacked self-discipline. He was uncontrollable. Anything the little boy inside of him wanted done, he did. As to Lily's comment, I knew that she mused over it for days. She told me that she pictured him as he sat on his million dollar sofa huddled with his people. It was three-weeks before the midterm elections. Lily said there were two things that he might've objected to: Number one was when she wrote that he had ill-gotten properties. Number two, he revealed his true nature. When Lily said don't let organized crime rule America, at those wee-hours of the morning, music from *The Godfather* should've played in the background at Pliartrum's retreat. Who was in the room, she wondered? Was his post a reply to what Lily wrote? If so, what was Pliartrum's reaction to it? Why did he write about Jewish Americans?

Pliartrum was guaranteed a dubious, but prominent place in the history books of the future for his audacious shenanigans in the White House. His presidency in history books will go down as the greatest fluke in American History. There was nothing compared to his outrageousness. His actions demanded that future historians found him impossible or irresistible to ignore. He needed to be studied as much, if not more, than leaders like Hitler or Napoleon, namely, all of the crooked crackpot leaders in World History. Lily demanded action. She wrote to newspapers about her comment and the Pliartrum post. She believed it exposed his true nature; his link to Organized Crime.

Chapter 12

My stint in the armed forces perplexed me. On the one hand, unbeknownst to me, *m-workers* frequently intervened so my uncontrolled behavior continued. On the other hand, *Mead* started the countdown. I was placed under a great deal of pressure; both physically and mentally. I was freed under certain conditions. *Mead* had sent word down on me. At each level there was complete agreement. The *m-workers* fashioned a noose, which was, on *Mead's* orders, tightened around my neck to get my attention. Instantaneously, it loosened and I was allowed to breathe for the moment. Meanwhile, the *m-team* activated the seed, which was planted inside all of us. In ninety-nine percent of us it lay dormant; it never saw the light of day. Once activated, however, it moved into my brain and it rapidly removed any sense of well-being; if there was any to begin with…

After high school it was, mainly, the trouble I should've been in for all of my cannabis use when it was illegal in the military or elsewhere. Once again, it happened without the trouble that I should've been in. I carried a matchbox with a piece of hash inside my uniform pocket. The aroma from my daily use filled the room I lived in at the barracks; it should've easily been detected with a simple sniff; it never happened. I went home on two occasions while I attended AIT for the Navy. I resupplied and bought another ounce, courtesy of Bobby. I flew home and then returned with it to the base. In basic training, as I said, I buried it under the building. At AIT, I kept it in my locker in the barracks. Nothing ever happened; there were never any consequences. Any authority's sense of smell was blinded by *Mead*. The *m-workers* ensured no odor reached anyone's nasal passages. Even the drug-sniffing dogs, if there were any.

I was free to move on; however, I had no plans. I never needed to make any as I saw later. I acted on impulse. But, I judged my impulses. Sometimes they were inappropriate. I knew right from wrong when it came to certain acts. I was tested again and again. I never knew that it was *Mead*.

My next endeavor, gradually, presented itself. All of my illegal activities were done on a whim. So, later, it never surprised me when I applied this same approach and attitude to all of my activities. I never put much thought into anything that I did in those years. I was still very impulsive. While in the navy, my whims were frequent. After I was discharged from the service, no thought was generated about my future. I whimsically chose California as my permanent residency when I filled out a form one day. Later, I picked a location that I lived at and the community college that I attended in my freshman year of college. I chose it, without contemplation, in the exact same manner. I graduated from college. I earned my Bachelor's Degree in Liberal Arts, which meant that I obtained a four-year degree for my future, and for no other reason. I needed the piece of paper to advance. I earned my piece of paper but I got something else in the process; it was totally unexpected. A change occurred. I was placed on a new path. A major transition headed my way.

All I knew was a new career path was chosen for me. Decades later, I reported it was an honor and a privilege; frankly, because I never deserved it. The sequence of events which led me to the path, however, was complicated and convoluted. I learned, but I educated myself the hard way. I was to earn my highest degree from *Mead*. It started with the most important lesson that I've learned up to that point. My entire behavioral structure needed correction. I never stole anything after it. I became totally honest; it was as if my life depended on it. My world turned around, but only in relation to my career, which was neatly woven, by *Mead,* into the fabric of my own personal problems.

I figured it out many years later. *Mead* decided that I was, finally, stopped. The *m-watchers* gave specific instructions to the *m-workers*. There was one last criminal impulse initiated in me just for such a purpose. After all of these years, I was caught. However, it was important that no criminal record existed, but that I learned my lesson. No more nefariousness. But, m-*workers* knew it was only accomplished if they hit me hard. So, *they* waited. It was tied to something important. Soon, the *m-team* had it all scheduled. They had the location, date, time, and criminal offense all set up, and when it happened it impacted me in a heartbeat.

It was for petty theft, which carried with it a citation and a fine. It was not a misdemeanor, and I never appeared before a judge. I learned, later, *Mead's* reason. When I was interviewed for a job, it was important that I said with honesty: "I have no criminal record - no misdemeanors or felonies, and I've never been in jail." It was true, physically, I never was. In my mind it was a totally different story. *Mead's* countdown began…

It was two-months before I graduated and earned my Bachelor's Degree. For once, I made future plans. I wanted religious study, believe it or not. I wanted to live and work in a Kibbutz in Israel. I applied for a fellowship. It required a sponsor. I made an effort to find one. It was imperative that I had an impeccable record of experience and achievement. I knew I met all of the qualifications. I wanted to go badly. I never knew or understood why. I just wanted to do it. Next, I, unknowingly, waited as *m-planners, m-developers* and *m-coordinators* prepared the crime. It was set, and it met all the criteria. The salvo which opened my future was harsh. I felt degraded. Especially two-months before graduation. I stepped into despair. But without all the trappings of actually being incarcerated. Mead insisted that I learned the hard way. I rarely filled out a job application so I never knew at the time that employers want to see criminal history, not arrests which led to nothing. For the fellowship, it asked only one thing: Have you ever been arrested?

I was between classes when I bought a pack of cigarettes in a vending machine. I didn't open them, I just put them into one of the pockets of my jacket. After my last class, as I remembered it, I went to the grocery store to buy something. As I stood in the express check-out with a grocery item in my left arm, the m-workers pulled their strings. Without a thought my right arm reached out to the cigarette rack, which they had in those days, and I shoplifted a pack of cigarettes. As I stood in the line, mindless, not a thought had gone through my brain. Cigarettes were very cheap in those days. Even so, a plain clothed security employee stood behind me the whole time and witnessed the crime. He caught me outside the check-out. He told me that he arrested me because I shoplifted a pack of cigarettes. I was handcuffed and awaited an Officer. I was taken to the small police station. Nobody else was there; it was just him and me. The officer took the handcuffs off. I was finger-printed and photographed. The officer who arrested me then completed a form. He asked me many questions. I answered honestly, all except for one question, are you a homosexual, he asked? I answered, in a deep voice, that I was not.

I never followed the words but they came directly from *Mead* through the Old Testament passage. I read it. I understood it. I heard it, loud and clear, but I ignored it. I still sought sexual activity with my own gender. I hardly ever got any. I never wanted friendship. And love was a foreign word that I knew nothing about. To me it was just about sex.

I received a citation. I was fined seventy-five dollars. I was driven back to the store, by the officer, where my car was illegally parked. I had a second citation under one of my windshield wipers for that violation as well. Mead's reconstruction project destroyed me for a period of time. As soon as I got back to my dorm room I tore up my fellowship paperwork. I cried into my pillow that night. *Mead and the m-team* knew; it hit me really hard. Decades later, I found out that the judge's office which housed my mugshot and record was burned to the ground. No, it wasn't me. Who else?

My future started in the business world, but it was not a good fit. I struggled a great deal with, unbeknownst to me, mental illness. Later, I looked back, and I believed that I should've figured it out a long time ago. I grew up in the 1960s, mental illness was largely unknown; even the mention of it was taboo. If someone in the family was mentally ill back then, it remained a secret even to the one who had it. *M-workers* followed what was ordered. They had discretion. But they were ordered under certain circumstances to do remarkably good things; miracles. And, at the same time they were ordered and carried unimaginable evil. I wondered, sometimes, how the horror was tolerated and how it smeared the Human Race as a whole. The evil and wicked elements which existed inside of each of us, some to a much higher degree, and some to a much lower one. It challenged us. Paths led to nowhere were a common practice of *m-developers.* Humans had ample opportunity to do the right thing. They also had ample opportunity to screw up. The data was collected and it was kicked up the chain of command to a kind of war-room where everything, of consequences, was decided.

My first job was interrupted by a car accident. It was two-years later. It occurred while I was on the job. It was not my fault. I broke my leg, and I received worker's compensation. Later, I resigned from the business world. My long awaited and desperately needed guidance from *Mead* and the *m-team* was now installed. I slummed around until my unemployment benefits ran out. My worker's compensation ended months ago. I lived with Ellen. She didn't want me there at first. I remembered, like it was yesterday, when she came home from work. I opened the door at the same time she stuck her key in. She paused, looked at me up and down and said: "How long are you here for?" From her tone and expression she wasn't exactly thrilled about me being there. But, as it turned out she let me stay. She and Dad had divorced a few months earlier after thirteen-years of marriage, and he had recently moved out. It was a small apartment, but Ellen tolerated me a whole lot more than Dad ever did.

Later, I understood why, and why I went into the navy. I didn't dream. I wished for nothing. There were no goals. I was so wrapped up in my nefariousness my brain never processed anything good and wholesome. Nothing was worthwhile and deliberate after I gave it any thought. My hopes and desires never materialized because I never put any effort into it. For example: Dad's real-estate business was simply the fulfillment of a dream of his. He conjured and wished that he made a lot of money. And, for a short period he did. But soon, like any dream, it ended for him.

I didn't like the business world. I never felt good about it. But, I had no other future planned. I had no other direction to go in. I had a piece of paper. It showed that I had earned my four-year Bachelor's Degree. But, my sites weren't aimed and ready to fire. Forget a vocation, it challenged my nefarious nature. Even though I never shoplifted again. The nefarious streak was still in me. I thought of the possibilities. The travel industry; no free plane rides or cruises to manipulate. Certainly not the banking industry; no free money or loans to steal. Real estate, no way. I'd be terrible in the Corporate World as well? Maybe as a teacher? An accountant? A trucker? A violinist? A swindler? A thief? An embezzler? A hitman? It was none of the above. *M-watchers* identified an attribute that I possessed. I really never knew it. In the data collected over many decades, my vocation was set by *Mead* and the *m-team*. I was to have a career in mental health.

Chapter 13

Glenda was the force for evil in the family. She kissed Mom's ass as she shamed me for something I should've gotten some help over. As a child I remembered that I acted out as a result. Two incidents came to mind. Both involved Glenda. Both were to shame and humiliate me.

The first one involved my dresser drawer; it was before Glenda left me the envelope with the marijuana inside. I had taken a knife and carved words into one of the drawers. It read something like: *This is my chest you can't take it. Leave my chest alone.* As soon as Glenda saw it she told Mom. I was whipped with a leather strap that night because my sadistic sister wanted to see me suffer.

The other time was when she caught me as I masturbated. I was about eleven, and she told Mom, who told me: "You'll get pimples," and when I did she humiliated me for every zit I ever had. She sang songs about it. She'd laugh out loud. Her love for hate was something I never understood. It's one of the things so prevalent in society. On air, she's the queen of hate. She made no bones about it. To her it was a badge of honor. Night after night, guest after guest, Glenda was nothing but pro-Pliartrum, and that the other side was filled with evil. She wanted the other side to squirm. She wanted them to report how terrible she was. It was all free press, and in her mind, just like Pliartrum and his family, each awaited their turn as the center of attention. My sister, the star who had a bank account that rivaled some countries, didn't have enough. She wanted more.

She saw Rich Pliartrum, Jr. the former president's number two son, for the first time at a Country Club Party event that showcased Pliartrum's retreat in Pennsylvania. Back then, when he was still president, and it was all at the taxpayers expense, that little shindig alone cost hundreds of thousands of dollars. That wasn't the worst of it. Pliartrum milked the coffers of this country like a dairy farmer. The cow was Bubba. Pliartrum, his family, and all of his real-life, genuine, died in the wool, Country Club Party members, played Bubba like a fiddler. His fans followed him like he was Peter Pan and they were off to Neverland; the children didn't want poverty or adulthood. They wanted to remain rich, not grown-up and poor; no matter what, they would remain rich. He hooked them like a fisherman's whose mouth watered profusely as he reeled in a trout for dinner that night. They weren't real Country Club Party members. Bubba controlled the Country Club Party, and the authentic Country Club members were deathly afraid of them. They were "animals," Glenda's were her words in private. She said that those were Pliartrum's words as well. Sometimes, Glenda told Pliartrum how to handle something. It surprised me when I learned how much she spoke to him. They were on speed-dial.

Rich, Jr. had been a guest on Glenda's show a number of times over the past few years. So when they met, for the first time, in person, she hit him. She hit him hard. The former president's number two son left his wife and five children for Glenda. They grabbed the headlines as the "power couple." The press, especially Glenda and her kooky news network, never got enough Pliartrum. The reason was as clear as

Lake Tahoe, he's been so good for business. Pliartrum made a lot of people a lot of money. Glenda benefited when she had fallen into the good graces of her potential new father-in-law even before she connected with Rich, Jr. The former Commander in Chief characterized her as the voice of reason. He blessed Junior's divorce, and welcomed Glenda into the fold, unofficially, because Glenda had her limitations as per her contract. She never campaigned for the former guy when he ran. She offered a hell of a lot of advice, which Pliartrum, "took seriously," I was told.

Glenda and I never saw eye to eye. Our dichotomy can best be explained when it came to the day that Dad left the family. My father gave up a lot of things throughout his life, and not just wives and children. He gave up on fatherhood because he never wanted it. He and Ellen never had children even though she was only in her mid-twenties when they were married. Dad died a pauper. After his death she told me that he was forced to marry Mom. My grandmother Annie insisted. She told Dad that he must be married to Mom. It was an edict and she merely passed it on. She was used by *Mead*. For whatever reason, *Mead* ordered it.

It was night time. Dad wanted to see us. It was just weeks after their split. Mom said that he wanted to talk to us. She put her foot down, however. She refused to let him come into the house. So, Glenda, Lily and I sat in his car. Frank was too young. Mom refused to let him see his father. Glenda sat in the front passenger seat. Lily and I sat in the back. Dad actually cleared his throat before he delivered his eulogy to the family. He told us that he found somebody else that he loved, and he wanted her. He said that he never wanted to live with Mom again. Lily lowered her head into one of her hands; she seemed saddened. Glenda 's expression showed that she felt rejected. She gave him her "how dare you" look. Dad noticed it and I saw that he lowered his head, for half a second, in shame. I think she wanted to shame him because, as she saw it, she was being rejected from her position as the first child. Or some other slight she fancied. I, on the other hand, felt nothing. I wasn't happy about it. But, I wasn't saddened either. It never phased me. He was never missed. I never hoped or wished that he came back though. He meant nothing to me.

Chapter 14

When Frank reached Boris' bedroom door he hesitated. "Signs flashed red," he said to me. He was being warned. He debated for a few seconds, then he carefully placed the padlock on the door, "where it should've been," he admitted to me.

"I took it off a week ago because he said he would have done better if it wasn't there. "But," he added: "Before I brought the padlock together and locked it, he tried to open the door."

"What the hell's going on? What are you doing?" He frantically pulled at the doorknob. He brought the lock together, and it closed. "Why are you doing this to me? I haven't done anything wrong!" He, repeatedly, banged on the door with his fists.

"I locked him in his bedroom, and then I called the police," he told me. "Our suspicion sprang up when he denied even knowing of the old lady. We all knew of her.
When the police arrived he had calmed down. The officers asked Frank if he ever had any guns in the house. He replied: "No guns." He paused and thought and remembered: "He owns a hunting knife." Two Police Officers had their guns drawn as they made their way down the hall. Frank slowly approached the door and he knocked.

"Yes," the disturbed son calmly answered.

"Boris, the police are here. They want to talk to you."

"Why do they want to talk to me?"

Frank looked at one of the officers; he shook his head.

"They're canvassing the neighborhood. They need to talk to everyone."

"Is that why you locked me in?"

One of the officers had a loud, deep and commanding voice. "We want you spread out on the floor, face down, understand?"

There was a second of silence before he said: "Yes, sir."

Frank unlocked the padlock and removed it. The officer with the deep voice pushed the
door open; its hinges creaked. Boris was face down; he spreaded out as if he just made an angel in the snow. "Where's the knife," one officer asked?

"What knife," he asked.

"The hunting knife," the Officer replied.

"I sold it," he said. Frank covertly looked at the other Office; he very lightly shook his head side to side.

The officer frisked him, cuffed him and then stood him up.

"Am I being arrested," he asked?

They each took one of the sixteen-year-old's arms and led him out of the room.

The interrogation room was cold and compact. The ceiling was low. The light was bright above the interrogated head of Boris; it made his shaggy red hair shine. From the teenager's claustrophobic expression the length and width of the room intimidated him. His juvenile eyes darted every-which-way as he looked for the camera. He sat in a hard chair which was bolted to the floor. He sat erect. His hands folded together in front of him as if he was a very good boy.

Detective John Wicks was a seasoned interrogator with a very professional manner. He introduced himself, cordially, to the young man seated in front of him. His words formed sentences as if he was a graceful ballerina; he danced divinely. He was a master of his art. He strung words together and delivered them in a manner that commanded transfixed attention.

I watched the interrogation on Youtube, because I never understood my nephew's motive. I needed to get inside of his mind. I never understood his pathetic path. Why was he on it? What put him there? Boris knew right from wrong. He took away a life. It was an unspeakable crime. Another said: "When a person hits the age of ninety, they must be a pretty good person. Centenarians, even more so." Why did Boris desire the death of a ninety-year-old woman? What wedged in his mind and kept the crack open in himself? Why did it widen? Boris decided to play the "I don't know what you're talking about card."

Detective Wicks had seen it all. He decided to roll-up his sleeves. There was a long night ahead. He called his wife before it started because already he knew. "You don't need to stay up. I'll be late." He ended the call. He read the investigators report. There were no witnesses. The crime took place at the time of day most people worked. The report outlined the crime scene investigation. It was classified as first-degree murder. "It was a crime of rage," the news reports announced. An expert, who was interviewed said: "It had a vindictive and twisted evil to it. The killer read, looked and listened to morbidity. It pushed him out of his fantasy world. He acted it all out, in his mind, exactly what he wanted to do. He already responded to internal stimuli a great deal about it. He was now motivated and prepared. He commanded it. He yearned for it in his heart. He swished fantasy's around in his mind for months. He felt good when he did it. He possessed the evil power of a sadist. But, Wicks decided to play to the boy's hubris.

He asked the young man: "Tell me what you know about assassins." The word brought out a kind of sensuality in Boris' eyes. Wicks knew that the youth lived in a world where only monsters felt comfortable. Wicks felt it wise, so he bypassed the "you'll feel much better if you confess," approach. He also sidetracked on the "do you want people to think you're a monster?" Lastly, the interrogator decided to nix the "there's two sides to every story. I want to hear yours." Wicks used those tactics before, and in that scenario he said things like: "Maybe it was an accident. Maybe it was in self-defense." No, the detective had been around long enough. He grasped the depths that the human mind sunk to, sometimes. He understood evil. He saw its power as he worked. He noticed how the mind sickened when fed a steady diet of misinformation, horror, and criminality. Wicks knew about the hands, which reached into a young person's mind. It was to be massaged. It was mentored. It was to be peppered with the spices of evil.

Boris was told that his mother feared him, and he smirked. He expressed intense interest when told he had the pulse of an assassin according to his medical information. Boris bought into it. He said: "The way you look at the world is the way you see it." Wicks granted the youngster permission and he hopped aboard a lane only the assassin took. He confirmed the high level of importance that he had placed on himself. The kid loosened up. He became more animated. He explained that he looked at humanity through a special lens. One only he accessed and controlled. He was a master, but he never acknowledged that he was the killer of a ninety-year old woman, at home, with her television on.

Wicks knew what he was up against. He felt it necessary to feed the boy's ego. For hours he answered questions. Wicks was tireless to the end. He worked on the boy just like a great artist worked on a painting; a little bit at a time. He gained the confession of the young man. He was some kind of superstar. Once into the suspect's mindset he asked Boris why he was so proficient at what he did. He replied that he never understood what he learned and why he learned. He answered that he read about military training. Along with his interest in the martial arts. It got him to talk about what he was interested in? Television, movies, videos and video games? The youngster professed his knowledge.

"It was just mental focus. I've studied things that I should've not studied." He boasted that no one taught him anything.

Wicks wondered, out loud: "Where did you learn to stab like that?"

"I didn't," he admitted. Wicks wanted him to explain the technique he used when he stabbed. He replied: "It was nothing fancy." He told Wicks that somewhere in the subconscious of his mind he developed the skills of an assassin, but, "with no training." The knowledge just came to him, he said.

I concluded that his mind and heart were sickened by the sort of proclivities he was exposed to in his environment. *Mead* quantified his data. The young man flirted with darkness. He consciously chose evil. And it was all due to the fact his *m-planner, m-developer* and *m-coordinator* had him pegged for an institutional life behind bars."

Chapter 15

Manuel's tendency to quibble with every word that Lily uttered became a warning sign that her adoptive son built a resentment that led to severe friction between the two of them. Lily was never mean or mad; it just wasn't her way. As a teacher she captured her student's hearts with her words, tone and manner. Power wasn't important to Lily, but she gained it anyway because of the way she disarmed all that she encountered. Manuel's mental acuity told her that despite his background, before the age of four, in her mind, he flourished. She believed that she'd set him free from the maltreatment he experienced, and she provided him with all of the love and attention he needed.

Before the boy reached ten, Lily had only one telltale sign that there was something wrong. It was when he was paddled at school. The boy never forgot it. Later, I thought that it had tripped the wire.

 Otherwise, he had a dream book childhood. He vacationed every summer with his Mom. They both loved animated movies. They watched them together regularly, especially the Disney films. Their living room wall was filled with framed photos. My favorite picture of them was when they went to *Walt Disney World* in Florida. Lily was big on history, too. Especially America's. She took Manuel to visit many historical sites. They took a trip to Gettysburg, Pennsylvania. They stood on the historic battlefields and toured the museum. Next, they toured the nation's capital. Lily wanted Manuel to be happy and she loved him very much. But she wanted him informed. He learned and understood just what democracy was. She thought that he was too young and spared from the politics, so he never learned of the perversion perpetuated by Pliartrum against the Constitution, Democracy and against the American people. Lily knew if the extremist ever got their way it would be the Confederate States of America, again, something they attempted to install back in the mid-nineteenth Century. Lily fought hard for the blue side. She wrote a blog, which encouraged the Anti-Pliartrum Party, or otherwise known as the People Party. She wanted voters to nominate Pliartrum's nephew, Horace Pliartrum as the opposition leader to the Country Club Party.

"I wanted him as the nominee because he was an eminent psychiatrist who stood up to his uncle when he was elected and won the Oval Office." Lily believed the former president's nephew, Horace, had the chutzpah to stand up to his uncle and organized crime. Horace described his kin as a tyrant. He referred to him in his book, as the deadliest threat to this democracy since the Civil War.

Lily wasn't all politics, however. She had friends. She had a life. She was generous with her time and money. She helped out whenever and wherever she could . She wanted to instill those traits, along with strong moral values, steadfastness and ethos into Manuel.

The honeymoon lasted for years. The boy was loved and he received everything he wanted with one exception that I remembered. He wanted to wear sneakers to his first day at kindergarten. Lily had bought a really nice outfit and shoes to wear but the clothes didn't match the sneakers. Manuel didn't listen to reason, so Lily ordered him to take his sneakers off, and to put on the new shoes. The boy never let it go, she said. When he reached his adolescentes he wore nothing but sneakers, even when he wore a tie and jacket. He started to rebel in other ways as well. Lily said that he talked back. He took no advice from her. He defied her, constantly. She talked to him about it, and, sometimes, he listened. But, it was all an act; deep down a cauldron boiled.

It was on one particular day that she stoked the fire and, possibly, paid a price for it. Manuel and Lily had another "fight." It started when he manipulated her for money, and he stole a credit card from her purse. He charged up three-thousand dollars as a runaway. He wined and dined and stayed at a fancy hotel for three-nights. When he came home his temper flared when confronted with what he did.

"He," she said, "quickly escalated." His expression and words shifted from meekness, with more lies and excuses, and words like please… Mom…, to fuck-you, bitch. I don't give a fuck what you say. He looked, and pointed his finger at me, like he had been crossed, she said. There was a high level of vengefulness in his eyes. They pushed, shoved and threw things at each other. Lily told me that he grabbed her arm and yanked at it with a sadistic look in his eyes. The bone snapped. She cried out in agony. She looked up and he yelled at her; "it's your fault!"

Suddenly, it was like he shifted gears. He melted like butter on a hot biscuit. His anger lifted. His eyes changed. He looked at her with compassion and remorse. He turned himself around quicker than an eggbeater. He drove her to the hospital. He cried and apologized all the way there and all the way back home. But, with Lily now in a cast she believed that he must face consequences. She unfolded her case at the kitchen table. In a cast, she explained that he needed to help himself; it was time for him to grow-up. Apparently, sometime ago, he stopped taking antidepressants, and he used marijuana. She knew it but she was blinded to do anything about it. *Mead*, again. Any substance abuse fueled his fire, which Lily understood. It was both genetic and environmental. He was born into it. Before the age of four he lived in hell. She lifted him out of it for the remainder of his childhood with the help of love and psychotropic medications. But it was just a *bandaid* on a gaping wound. Lily never learned of his behavior in high school. "He was a nice guy," someone said from his school, "until you crossed him." Lily did more than that, she threw him out and told him that he could not come back until he stopped the marijuana and started taking his antidepressants again. He stayed with friends only two-weeks before it was accomplished...

However, it interested me to read amongst her documents that she had a file about our Uncle Stu, who was my mother's brother. He had quite an entanglement with Lily over her comment about Pliartrum. She shared the comment she wrote about Pliartrum with him. Her relative was pro-Pliartrum and he wrote back with an angry response, the last line of which was threatening. "I wish you all the best." Lily wrote that it sounded like a mob send-off.

Chapter 16

Detective Wicks signed the interrogation paperwork necessary to send Boris to juvenile detention. The young man stayed there until his trial. The boy hadn't a clue about life. He refused to conform to societal norms. But no one imagined how strong ASPD was in this kid. Frank made an effort in the beginning. He spoke fondly of fatherhood, once married. He once said: when he had a family that he would be a good dad. He had delusions, I thought. He said that he and Boris would always be together as the boy grew up. He said he wanted Boris to have the ability to say that he was always there for him. He wanted his son as his best friend. He said he wanted to lead him through all of life's battles.

Pat took to the bottle throughout the day. Following Boris' placement into juvenile detention the family felt relief, Frank told me. But Pat pissed him off. She always promised she wouldn't drink in the daytime. She broke it time and again. She still cared about him, however, because he was her first and only true love. Although, her *m-workers* were on alert.

They compiled enough data, on a serious matter, for the *m-watchers* to take note. It was reported to the *m-team*: Pat still thought that Frank didn't love her anymore, after they had reconciled. Later in life, she revolted and drank even more.

Frank did not help matters. He became another person. Suddenly, he was filled with hate and cynicism all the time. President Pliartrum had just lost reelection, Frank was radicalized by then. We argued about it over the phone. I worked in California, at a MH assignment, unknowingly, for *Mead*. The last time we argued, he hung up on me because I told him that Pliartrum was another Hitler. Like I said: "click." His reality was topsy-turvy; he had everything upside down. Glenda and PROX-NEWS brainwashed him, as well as the good members of the Country Club Party, and a large part of the American people, as a whole, and it was all because Pliartrum coveted power. He wanted organized crime to rule America.

M-watchers ordered *m-workers* who acted accordingly because within his heart were dreams. Some people really angered him. He was bittered and he hated humanity's diversity. He cheered for hate toward anybody who wasn't just like Pliartrum, with whom he identified. After he met Pat at the Legion and impregnated her, he said that he was ready for fatherhood. That was funny to me, the fact that he didn't really want the kid.

I blamed him and people like him who voted for Pliartrum and put him into power. It's all the king of fat asses ever wanted. Power meant everything to him. He always looked for more and more money. He gritted his supporters, especially Bubba, relentlessly. And they donated, again and again. They bought his t-shirts and his digital trading cards. He had millions of grandmothers and grandfathers who contributed to him every month. It was a recurring charge that came out of their debit accounts. The bigshot Country

Club Party members contributed as well, or else. It allowed Pliartrum to milk senior citizens. To bleed them dry, if necessary. The ill-informed, the uneducated, the simple minded were also manipulated. That and the extremists were to make up the Country Club Party coalition; it took the party into the future against the "evil" People Party.

Frank knew that Pliartrum followed the Fuhrer's playbook. He, and tens of millions of other Americans were channeled into it by *Mead*. Then the tired old order came down. It was from the *Executives*. Mankind had, once again, learned nothing, and, as a result, once again, the World would be flipped into total turmoil. It occurred every five or six generations, according to one, highly placed source, and every ten generations there's civil war, because the lesson had never been learned. Live in peace and in harmony. Tolerate others. Love thy neighbor. Warfare between countries, religions, races and ethnicities should've ended. Tribalization must be stopped before humanity ends on its own. It was possible. It happened in the 1970s when President Jimmy Carter was in Office. He brought two bitter foes together, Israel and Egypt. They made peace. They didn't like each other, but at least, they tolerated one another. They exchanged Ambassadors and started diplomatic relations. There was already enough conflict within a country's borders. Warfare within the family. It sprung from conflict within the self.

Mead and the *m-team* operated on humanity like a surgeon operated on an individual; both were very careful at what they did. It started with the family and genetics, as well as a newborn's upbringing, the environmental part, because mental illness stemmed from a sick-soul. As a regular guy, Frank was always grounded, just like Lily. He never left our hometown like me and Glenda. He grew up there and he lived there. He, frankly, became a goy. Everything about him screamed goyim. A Jewish man who hung out with Jew haters was complicit in their hate, I thought when I heard more about what was up with Frank.

He and his buddies: Keith, Don, Catch and Sammie, who all hung out in the basement at the bar. Five guys, whooped it up. They wore their dirty baseball caps, and stood around the bar keeping up with the latest Plairtum news. They all wore jeans and t-shirts. A hint of unmanliness would be a sign, I thought, of being unPliartrum. Either a People Party member, a fag, a lesbian, a transgender, or those who were of a different race and nationality. These men followed their leader who tolerated no one. Not even Lily, and her comment online meant anything to Frank, but to the fellows in the basement, and people like them, it was their turn to govern, which translated to; it's okay to hate. And they did, Pat emailed me. I wasn't on social media, so I never looked at Frank's *facebook* page. She told me that he was full of pro-Pliartrum propaganda. He was a MAWA leader of his block. He made sure that everyone in the neighborhood had a Pliartrum for President 2020 sign in the front yard. To Frank, MAWA was *Make America Wonderful Again*. I told him that it stood for *Make America White Again*.

Frank told me, when we still spoke, that he admired Pliartrum for his honesty. He said things, in the manner, that his truth was the only truth, and that anybody else's truth was anti-Pliartrum. I thought of 1930s Germany as he continued. He rattled off the Fuhrer's wish list, he wanted the weeds rooted out of their society. I reminded Frank that he's Jewish and that the people who he associated with, amongst others, were trapped like they were on the Titanic and Pliartrum was the captain. I reminded him of the young German commercial airline pilot for Lufthansa, who crashed the airliner, with a hundred plus passengers, into the side of a mountain. They were, instantly, disintegrated. That's what Pliartrum was doing to him, I explained. He rattled off some shit about the current president's son and about his crimes. I know he watched Glenda every night, and then called her after each show to tell her what he thought. Pliartrum's kids really face serious criminal consequences. They've always been mixed up in all of their father's crimes. Frank was not simple minded, yet he got into bed with them. He rolled around in the covers; he was stimulated by Pliartrum. They had no offerings of goodness toward their fellow man, rather they grovel to Pliartrum. Good Country Club Party members were afraid of him. Frank loved him. He, in his *Godfather* way of putting things, had them all scared to death of him. *"He made them an offer they couldn't refuse."* Pliartrum, his enablers, Frank and his buddies broke bread with Holocaust deniers, racists, and people who profited off all of the hate. He and the others demanded their way of life. I sighed and thought: *Mead*. When will mankind learn the lesson?

Chapter 17

It was my career path. A path that I never walked upon either for myself or to the benefit of another. It was an honorable vocation, but, sometimes, gut-wrenching and tragic. I was frustrated, saddened and challenged by it, but at the same time invigorated. Time passed, and through it, I watched magic as it worked on souls weakened by mental illness; my own being one of them. I learned many lessons both on and off the job. The career was meant for me. It fit me like a glove. Day or night and even in some of my dreams, my new vocation, which I was unprepared and uneducated for, unfolded. However, deep down, I never knew it, but I was very natural at it. My new career addressed my depressed inner-self that held up for so very long. It was a non-stop journey of enlightenment and tragedy; an education on goodness. But the road twisted and turned as I tried to get there. There were potholes and detour signs. All traffic lights turned red and obstacles were placed on the path. And, later, at times, it went down an endless road of misery and pain.

My life was upended numerous times. An edict was issued through *Mead*, which meant higher authority had been consulted. I forged a path into the volatile world of the human mind and human behavior. It was both wonderful and nightmarish; the secrets held by the soul. From the deepest part of hell to the highest cloud in heaven, I cleared the branches that clouded my vision into life. What I discovered outdid everything that I lost. I faced an arduous and laborious journey up steep mountains, and across great deserts and vast oceans. If I was incarcerated, I accomplished nothing; nothing good that is. I was humbled by this change because, as I saw it, either I went to my grave with nothing but regrets. Or, at my demise, I contributed to the good while I lived.

To start the fantastic journey I needed, as I said before, a Bachelor's Degree; it helped me get a job in the business world, but I knew nothing of what to do with it otherwise. *Mead* connected to the *m- team*. *M-workers* were ordered to begin. I started at the bottom of this new career field. Literally, I moved into a cheap basement apartment of an old Victorian home. I noticed across the street there was a stretch of old fashioned rowhomes, the kind that had great porches on them. One, in particular, stood out. Quite a number of people came and went through its door. It happened throughout the day. I took a breath of fresh air when I emerged from the cellar. I picked up a newspaper at the corner store. There was no high-tech in those years. I went to the help wanted ads. I was in poor shape, both physically and mentally. My only job experience was as an administrative worker. I found an ad for a clerk typist. I knew right away that I qualified for the job. I also had that four-year degree, which I had planned on and obtained because I thought that I needed it. However, at this point and time, the degree meant nothing. In fact, if I revealed it when I was interviewed they probably wouldn't have hired me, because with my degree I could be doing fifty other different things.

The help-wanted ad listed an address to apply at. It was directly across the street; it was that home that I saw all of the comings and goings. I looked across the street at it. A sizable *Stars and Stripes* was attached outside the home. There was a big blue placard sign on the wall next to the entry-way. It read: *Meyer's Club - where friendship begins and loneliness ends.*

I was hired for the clerk typist position in the administrative office of a MH program for chronically mentally ill adults who lived in the community. The Meyer's Club was a long-standing social service agency. It was started in the 1960s, it provided therapeutic programs for social, recreational and life skills to adults with mental illness.

I remembered when I first crossed the threshold of its door. I had no idea that I had entered the MH world. I couldn't even fathom that it was my home for the next thirty-five years, and beyond. I had arrived at where I established my career, and even more importantly, it established a path. I attempted to do better; somehow I was made aware, and my inner-self and physical-self connected, and I was supplied with information. I taught the very thing to many MH clients at my last job when I was a Therapeutic Rehabilitation Specialist. I explained that our inner-self, the soul, and the physical self were together and we were united as one. If there was conflict between self and soul, then there was a split. A division, which I told them happened. My words echoed a World War I slogan, which I repeated often: *United We Stand. Divided We Fall.* It wasn't too long after I started that I recognized that I had mental illness. I understood that I was depressed. I sought help outside the club. Time passed and I thought that I got better, because I responded to the antidepressant medication. But much later, I learned the hard way; the brain altered drug never lasted. I only put a *Bandaid* on a nasty wound.

I remained the clerk typist for about two months. One day I borrowed the ear of a very nice man. He was the Executive Director of the Meyer's Club. "I'd like to work with the members," I said. He permitted it. I gave up the clerk typist position to become a therapeutic-recreation program-developer. Translation: I started my MH career from the very bottom.

The way I thought that I saw myself, years later, was that I listened to the ignored. I heard them and responded to them with empathy and goodwill. I had a way with me. I never realized it, but I had a calm bedside manner; it was like I was a medical doctor while I worked. When there was any kind of conflict, within people's self or with others, I lowered the temperature. For the first time in my life I felt respected. When I worked with my peers I learned along with them. I was the inept one. I was the one who never had a real friend. I had a lot of problems, and when I looked back I benefited from my occupation.

I felt comfortable there. I recognized it as my career early on. I admitted, to myself, that I understood that I had a problem, and that I was on the right path to find the answers that I sought. I had a few extra layers of compassion. Maybe it was because I was one of them, although I never talked about it or me. Something hit me, however, on my first day on the job. It was so beautifully choreographed, by *Mead*, as I looked back at it. I was cleared for assignment. I was chosen. I worked with those who were diagnosed with a serious mental illness. I listened, watched and learned. Myself and two others staff members planned social, recreational and life skills programs, and carried them out. For the first few months I worked with the goodhearted people who were developmentally delayed.

They had programs like bowling at the Jewish Community Center. Feeding the ducks at the lake. Walking along the riverbank. Going to movies and restaurants. We had a conversation group. The list of wonderful recreational and social activities, combined with the teaching of life skills, made a big difference in their lives and in mine.

The months passed and there was turnover in the ranks. The adult MH therapeutic recreational coordinator gave notice and left the club. I applied for the position and I was hired. I accepted and embraced the world that I worked in, and that I knew, that I lived in, as well. However, it was at this point there was a problem. It was the life skills part. I knew nothing. I knew if I shoplifted that I would be caught, and if I stole anything else; it wasn't any different. I had no other lessons that I had learned. I had nothing to offer, so I learned as they learned. I presented skills from a teacher's manual. There was always a discussion on each topic we learned. When with the members, I socialized freely, for the first time in my life, but as the boss; it helped a lot long before I learned the naked truth. For the first time I felt comfortable around others and tolerated myself. Still, it was only when I worked. When I was home, I stayed to myself.

Over a span of thirty-years, I worked in MH. Both on the job and off, it was all MH. I even dreamed about it. I never knew that I had only two-years at the club, before I moved on to other MH assignments. My path included a new tool that *m-workers* installed in me; the cluster headache entered into my life. *M-worker*s were ordered, at first, that I be awakened each night with tremendous pressure and powerful pain in my brain. It stabbed me repeatedly in the same eye, forty, fifty, sometimes sixty minutes or more. The pain felt like it was inflicted by an icepick. The source of it remained unknown to the medical world. It took me decades until I understood; it was *Mead*. My life long overseer had only opened doors of criminality and deceitfulness. Nothing good was opened to me. When I made an effort toward the good; I was always stopped; it never worked out. Not when I was a kid. I recalled when I wanted to attend Hebrew School or *Yeshiva*. What I wanted was shot down. In fact, I remembered that Mom laughed when Pop-Pop said: "So, you wanna be a Yeshiva boy" he acted like he was in prayer, and he laughed. In fact, everybody in the room laughed except for me.

My religious needs were ignored. The fellowship that I tore up came from the heart. I wanted to live in Israel, pending my graduation from college. I recalled how I reasoned. It was because of the shoplifting lesson that I learned courtesy of *Mead*. It blocked me a third time, as well. My path toward religion was halted. As a kid I reached out to it, but I experienced a great void. My heart emptied, but it continued to beat even though it was bone dry. I remembered that I stepped back two-steps, but I never found the new path, and I never proceeded. I was frozen, religiously.

It was upon my departure from the club, that I moved right into another position. When I gave notice at a job and departed, there was a period of time that I never worked. It was down-time. But, as soon as I could, usually, two-years later, I bounced back, and when I did, I found a completely different job, although the positions, all except for two, were always in the MH field. I did fine for two-years or so, then, I petered out. I quit. I uprooted. I "traveled." I never understood. I knew zilch, but the *m-workers* worked overtime on me.

My lessons and punishment lasted for decades. Cluster headaches "traveled" along with me everywhere I went. Usually, for some people, it was nice to have a companion on a trip. I'd rather, at those times, been dead. But, I kept going. I "traveled" only with Rusty and my possessions. My dog was always by my side. And lucky me, the whole cycle repeated itself. There were four breaks, over thirty-years…

Each one lasted a couple of years. It took me to depths that I never imagined.

But, I always rebounded. Soon after I found employment again. It was another job. I worked in another capacity in the MH world. My MH transitions began at the Meyer's Club, two-years after I arrived. Suddenly, one day I had a whim, which I followed. I gave notice. I moved to another state. I left the club for no reason. I liked being there. People liked me and I liked them. But I moved on. I had a send off, and they gave me a beautiful gift, a very nice briefcase made of soft leather. In those two years I did things that I never did before. Things that were social. For example, once a month, I took a group of members to a nightclub where there was a live band. The members, me included, danced until the wee hours of the morning. Nobody drank alcohol, just sodas. The program was very well received. We also had educational and recreational programs. We traveled to Washington, D.C. to the Smithsonian Museums and the National Zoo. We traveled up to Mystic Seaport in Connecticut, where we toured an old whaling ship, and ate clam chowder at a chowder festival.

But, the lesson that I learned and relayed to myself was encrypted to me for the longest time. I packed up and moved to a town in another state. I was hired, rather quickly, for my first MH job after the club. I was a MH technician. I served SMI (seriously mentally ill) adults at the State psychiatric hospital in Las Vegas, Nevada. The patients were there, because they had a MH crisis. I followed orders from the psychiatric nurses. I spent most of my time out amongst the patients. Some slept in their rooms. I conducted a bed-check every fifteen-minutes. Others watched television, and some walked, slowly, back and forth through the hallways. The job was short because three months later, I was hired as a Teaching Parent Relief for the State residential treatment program for kids. In the second job, I worked with severely emotionally disturbed children aged seven to sixteen

But, I packed my bags four-years later. I moved on. Again, it was part of the cycle. I never understood or questioned the transitions. I determined, years later, that *Mead* gave me a taste of my own medicine when it came to the kids. The temptation to show me how, as a child, I treated myself and those around me. My behavior was very poor, because I was out of control. My mental health education was too tempting a morsel for *Mead* to pass up. I hated the transitions, sometimes. I, thankfully, finished my second stop on the tour. Having brought me into this line of work, *Mead's team* called the shots. I was on its MH tour, and it lasted for three-decades.

I held six-positions in three states. I was employed in a seventh and eighth job, but they weren't in the MH field. I learned, but then I suffered. I "traveled" for punishment not pleasure. For many months, over many decades, the cluster headache pain continued. Conveniently, when I was between jobs; it, got even worse. I "traveled" only in the spring and summer. These whims never came in the dead of winter. My downtime, in my warped mind, totaled forty-thousand miles, which was driven in three separate cars over the time span. Two of them looked like broken down junk cars. But they never broke down. They leaked a ton of oil. I carried a few quarts with me all the time. One vehicle's engine overheated. I'd have to pull over to put water into it. But, once I was in a traffic jam, on a freeway, as I drove out of San Francisco. The needle stayed at high. The traffic hadn't moved for minutes on end. I was frantic. I was sure it would break down. I had no air conditioning. The windows were down and it was in the middle of summer, and the needle didn't budge. It never went higher; but it never decreased. Me and Rusty worried. I surmised during this time there would be this nightmarish scene with me and

Rusty, stuck in the middle of a sea of motor vehicles. Thanks to *m-workers*, who worked regularly on automotive vehicles and their affairs, so the car never overheated to the point it broke down. It stayed at high for twenty or more minutes before the traffic crept ahead.

I had the road trips down to a science because I did it so often. I was always packed with all of my personal possessions, kitchen odds-and-ends, four large boxes filled with VHS tapes, a VCR, television set, a ton of clothes, and most importantly, Rusty. I went through state after state. I only stopped at night. I always had a room in a franchised establishment. Me and Rusty ate fast food all the time. I drove about five-hundred-miles per day. I never stayed long wherever I went. Pennsylvania to Nevada, to California back to Pennsylvania, then down to Florida, and back to Nevada once again. I repeated this process four-times, although I only went to the deep south of the continent once.

I received a Social Security disability check every month. I was diagnosed with depression. Before I "traveled" I saw a psychologist. I was back on psychotropic medications, which I had stopped. I moved to Florida for seven-months. I lived with, and tolerated, these zig-zag moves back and forth for endless hours and miles. I always "traveled" on the Interstate Highway System. I was all over the nation, and I was really tired. I pledged to myself; I moved no more. I settled in for a few years in different MH jobs. I broke my pledge and I was back on the road again doing the same things. Years later, I was accompanied by my nemesis, the cluster headache. It kicked my ass day and night. I hated life. However, my greatest contempt was saved for the attacks I had while I was driving. Those were all really bad. I cradled my head as I drove on. The pain was unbelievable and I wasn't doing myself any favors. At that time I smoked cigarettes, which only heightened the pain.

. After I resigned from my State position with SED kids. I was in poor physical shape. Cluster headaches happened day and night. I was still on Social Security Disability, but I was allowed to supplement the benefit. I worked a part-time job. Without doubt, I understood years later, it was *Mead* and his *team* who tortured me and facilitated everything. *They* laid out the blueprint for the next four years.

For the first two-years, I learned lessons hinged to MY homosexuality. The studio apartment that I moved into was a block away from the gay-bar district. The most popular drinking establishment sat next to a small video store. *Video Rentals* had regular movie VHS tapes to rent, but in the back there was a sizable array of heterosexual and homosexual pornographic VHS tapes to rent or buy. They had a help-wanted sign in the store's window. I was hired on the spot and I began the part-time job the next day.

M-planners, m-developers and *m-coordinators* had shifted into another area because I still hadn't learned my lesson about MY homosexuality.

The months I worked there were of educational value. *M-workers c*ollected a great deal of data, which showed that I was totally, socially, dysfunctional. I had a lot of sex, but there was no love. I cried over the phone to Frank about my problems, and how I felt as I worked there. I "traveled" again. This time it was short; only one-thousand miles. I returned to Las Vegas and the video store. Three months later I left their employment, and "traveled" again.

My new studio apartment was located in another area of town. I was well, mentally, and I became an elementary school substitute teacher. Two years later, I obtained another State MH position and left another noble profession back to another.

The reason I became a substitute teacher was because there was a State hiring freeze. In my first year, as a teacher, I struggled. I was overweight, and I had just recovered from the last grueling road trip; it criss-crossed the nation three-times. Granted, it was the longest one of them all. But I was hired as a substitute based solely on the fact that I had a Bachelor's Degree. It didn't matter what it was in. I had never stood in front of a classroom filled with children as an adult. I worked with mentally ill kids at my last MH job. But, it was different this time. I realized, years later, that I was like a star; all eyes were drawn to me because of my position as the teacher. Kids, I discovered, looked to adults for knowledge. They wanted more than the ABCs. At my last MH position I implemented the mentally ill children's individual treatment plans. Sure we tried to teach other things: self esteem, etc. In school, however, I learned that they looked for more than regular education.

It was during my first weeks, of being a substitute, that things went haywire. One day, I must have displayed non-verbal communication i.e. an expression that I was mad at something, It and along with my words, did the trick. I taught nothing good that day to the class of fourth-graders because those actions led to something bad. The kids placed a note on the desk when I wasn't looking that said: "We hate you." At the end of the day I wrote a note to the teacher about it. I felt hurt. It shook me. I must have processed it in my mind rather quickly because soon after I joined a gym things changed. One morning, when I showered something happened. A touch of wisdom came to me… I worked on it, relentlessly. As the excess weight melted off, I carried on, I built on the words and I ran them over and over in my mind… It became monumental.

I was assisted and I experienced a remarkable transformation. The weirdest thing was, years later, after I worked for the State with SED kids, I came home from another day at school. There was a young man seated on the concrete steps of my apartment building; he sat next to a ten-gallon aquarium. There was a sizable turtle in it. The young man called out: "Want a turtle." I remembered next that I heard: "You're, Ken Isaacs." He added, "You're looking good."

I looked at him with raised eyebrows and asked: "How do you know my name?" It turned out that he was one of the kids that I served when I worked at State MH with kids. It was ten-years ago, when he was thirteen. Immediately after he told me his name I remembered him. We shared a little conversation over the smoking of some marijuana in my apartment. Of course, if he was thirteen-years-of-age, I should've never smoked or given it to him the way Glenda gave to me, all those years ago. It was remarkable to see him. Firstly, he looked nothing like he did as a young teenager. It was funny because the image in my mind, at that time, pictured him as a boy. So as he sat in front of me it was a strange feeling knowing our history. He talked about his life. I knew the circumstances of how and why he entered the State's residential, behavioral program. He battled with life just like everybody did.

These were good times. I was in good physical and mental shape. Marijuana was back in my life, thank God, because the cluster headaches never left me. The plant was made by *Mother Nature*. It helped me cope with agony. I stopped smoking cigarettes, months ago, and replaced it with cannabis. The plant, as indicated before, helped me. Not everybody who had cluster headaches found that cannabis helped the condition. In one study, only twenty-five percent found it helped. On the other end of the spectrum there were twenty-five percent who reported that it made the headaches worse for them. While the majority of cluster headache people, fifty-percent, said that it made no difference at all. It didn't help them. But it didn't hurt. The pain went on. I used what worked, the cannabis, because I finally found a steady supplier. He was the first person that I bought it from on a consistent basis. Every time I needed it he was there. It allowed me to fight the torture. I started to turn the tables, and eventually, I gained the upper hand over them. I still got them, but I got rid of them quicker with the use of cannabis.

Mead, however, had new plans for me. The State had lifted its hiring-freeze. I was soon hired by another division within the State MH System. I became a psychiatric caseworker. I was given a caseload of chronically mentally ill adults who I worked with. I helped them with all of their business. Landlord problems, social security matters, trouble at the bank, etc. But, I also presented, to the clients, the States MH psychosocial rehabilitation program. I taught adults in groups. It was life skills training, and I added my little shtick, from the classroom, as I taught their program. I learned from the program that I taught. They were basic common sense topics: Socialization, communication, coping skills, etc. Eventually, I finished at that clinic. The collected data indicated that *Mead* had transitioned me again. This time it was an assignment at another clinic. I performed the same duties but, only weeks after I arrived, I ruined it or I should've said that *Mead* ruined it.

I had an episode that never happened to me before. I blew up. There were no clients at this brand new clinic I was assigned to. It was brand new. We weren't fully staffed yet. One day I sat at the front desk and I was bored. I remembered that I twiddled with a paperclip. In the course of it the *m-workers* took action. It was something that I did and said to a coworker. She told me that she hated the classical music that I put on in the waiting room. I bolted from my chair and I told her that she hated everything, and I stormed back to my office. The next day, I was told that I was being disciplined. Then, for the first time in my MH career, I lost it. I yelled out: "I quit."

Disturbed, I frantically went into my office and took down every drawing that the kids in the elementary schools had drawn for me. I was caked into my sickness. I threw the gifts out when I got home. They were a tool that I used. I had them tacked up all over the wall space, so when I met with clients for individual one on one psycho-social rehabilitation sessions I found they worked because they set the right tone. I cherished them very much. I never asked for them. In those two-years, I substituted, which followed the "we hate you," message, I turned it around. I received more than a dozen drawings from children at different schools from different grades and classes. They created personalized drawings and presented them to me. They thanked me, all in their own way, for being their substitute teacher that day.

After my flare-up, the next day, I had kidney stone blockage. I had an emergency surgery; it was unblocked that night. After I recovered the State allowed me to transfer to another clinic. I hadn't a clue what was going on with me. I knew that I had Graves Disease, and I took medication. I also knew that I was depressed. But, at that time I was not on an antidepressant, it ended only after I "traveled," again…

Back when the cluster headaches started, the Veterans Administration (VA), tried everything modern medicine developed to fight it. None of it worked on me. I was, frequently, absent during my last year with the State in their MH system. The cluster headaches assaulted me each night; it was really bad, and it happened so frequently, that I wanted to die. I quickly, mentally, deteriorated. My illness kept me away so often that I forfeited pay. I had used up all of my sick leave. I fell into a deep depression. In the last few months of my employment, my illness was so profound that I didn't shower. I had nothing to fight the cluster headaches with. I had a sick mind, in addition, but I wasn't connected to any MH services. I just worked at one.

Antidepressants were foreign to me for many years. Physically, I was a mess with my excess weight, a sick mind and the cluster headaches. However, mentally, it only got worse. One day, I was at home. I had called off again. The phone rang. It was somebody from the State Personnel office. The caller was unknown to me. She asked me why, the other day, was my car parked outside of a home that belonged to a client. There was a long pause… I knew nothing of *Mead*, all I knew was my shtick. *It* held all of the cards. And all the while, *they* worked, precipitously, behind the scenes. As *m-watchers* observed, *m-workers* guided the conversation and collected data. And by the end of the call, my demoralized mind uttered those two words that I used before: "I quit," and I hung up the phone.

Chapter 18

Glenda loved a good fight. She kindled one between Lily and former President Pliartrum. She rumbled, just like Pliartrum did when she mocked him:

"Who in the hell is Lily Isaac?"

And Lily replied: "Why did a former president of the United States of America write and post a remark in response, for all the world to see, to a simple comment left on Youtube by Jane Q. Public, who, again, simply watched a video, and offered her opinion..

"Our former fearless leader had no self control," she asked? "Any normal balanced person, in leadership, of the greatest nation in the history of the world, should not have entertained it in the first place. He should've, instantly, dusted it off. Or, it was never presented to him in the first place, because the former president's time was valuable, and it was never interrupted by an average citizen's comment on a Youtube video. "Poof, the comment went away, it never existed. Who cared about what someone in the public thought." In Lily's opinion: "There were no thoughts of the public, which should carry any weight in the eyes of the Leader of the Free World." But she got under his skin and gave him a sock-it-to-me.

"He does it all the time. I know when he's lying to me. I just say, okay, next question," Glenda told Mom. "He is a superb liar, " she added. "He knows that people know that he's a liar. He even lies to himself. So if I said the earth was round, he said the earth was flat. He convinced himself, automatically, that it was flat. And his words were never questioned." He repeated them again and again until it became fact.

Lily concluded: "The guy acted more like a tough kid in a rough neighborhood; he bullied his way to the top; he had everything that he wanted. He bullied his way through a pack of World Leaders once. The scene was when he elbowed his way to the front of the pack. He looked like a bully. Like a spoiled child, definitely, not the President of the United States."

Lily always had Pliartrum's number. "He was so damn obvious; he's a terrible actor," she said. The stupid inexperienced thug cracked. She said: "He was crooked before he took Office. He was crooked while in Office. And, he was crooked after it." While Glenda's opinions were quite the contrary. "He is a genius. I've never been around anyone like him, and I have been around everyone who glitters." Those were her latest public comments. Privately, she told Mom: "He's a big fat stupid liar in a nice suit."

Lily wondered who was in the room that night with Pliartrum? What was said before he posted his remarks? Why did he address it to Jewish Americans?

His retreats were for the rich. Gatherings of wealthy people where there he needed the energy. He boosted his fragile ego.

"It was like orgasm after orgasm to him", according to Glenda, "he's an ego-junkie; he needed a shot of it every ten-seconds. The lack of morality, empathy and conscious guilt showed that he entered this World without those features. His gluttony for money never abated." The guy would steal from your grandmother in a New York minute. He ruined lives. Families torn apart because of his politics. Responsibility for the death of more than one-hundred-thousand people who laid at his fat bone spurred feet. People died because of his presidential malpractice.

Pliartrum, by his actions, had guaranteed a place in the history books of the future for his audacious shenanigans in the White House, and why his presidency in United States history books will go down as the greatest embarrassment in the Country's history. There was nothing compared to his other outrageousness. His actions demanded attention and historians found him impossible and irresistible to ignore. He needed to be studied as much, if not more, than leaders like Hitler or Napoleon. Namely, all of the crooked crackpot leaders in World History. Lily demanded action. She wrote to newspapers about her comment and Pliartrum post. She believed it exposed his corruption and criminality, and that he was an illegitimate president because he should've been identified as a bonafide, one-hundred percent, died in the wool, crook. I understood because I knew one of those crooks.

—

My first memory of Uncle Stu was when he played the piano and sang "peanut butter," when we were young children. We were at Mom-Mom's house at a family gathering for a holiday meal. He was a young man in his early twenties then. I remembered that he always looked happy. I recognized later that he really loved life. But none of it was ever pointed at me. In fact, when Dad left the family Uncle Stu could've had a foot in the door to take over the mantle of male role model for me and Frank. He passed, we never saw the guy, and he just lived on the other side of town. He served no other purpose in my life. Nothing ever healthy or good happened whenever I saw him as I grew up. Once, I was wined and dined, at the racetrack, he delved into the intricate details of thoroughbred racing and how to pick a winner. He took a small pencil from his ear. He went through the *Daily Racing Form* with an eagle eye focus. He picked a gelding; it ran in the money twice. I picked a horse too and he gave me two-dollars to bet on it. I was sixteen-years old. I saw a posted sign which stated: twenty-one was the minimum age to gamble and make a bet. I went to one of the many gaming windows and made my bet. No problem. The place was packed with excitement. My adrenaline rushed, during each of the ten races on the card that Sunday afternoon. It screwed me up even more. I was hooked. Uncle Stu was hooked on it, too. And, casinos and Pliartrum.

Chapter 19

I was told that Glenda held Mom's hand at the time she took her last breath. Lilly and Frank stood by her side at the moment of her expiration. Pat reported to me that Lily fainted the moment my Mom took her last breath. When Mom died I was not by her side. I was at Frank's Patriot Park Home. I moved in, once again… They really grieved over Mom. When asked they spoke of their beloved mother who, sadly, had "passed away." I just said: "She died."

The cold weather met with gusty winds; it shook the naked trees as it rained. There were one-hundred-thirty-nine friends and family who came to the solemn affair. They each signed the book and paid their respects. The cemetery was large. There was row after row of headstones. It was cold inside the building that housed Mom's casket. There were a lot of benches. A sizable red carpet separated them down the middle. There was no comfort for anyone. Each person sat on a hard wooden bench. Inside were the many people who knew Mom during her lifetime. They were packed inside like sardines. In the front rows family members were split. On one side it was me, Lily, Manuel and Pat. Across the aisle was Aunt Glenda, Frank and Pat. I was in the poorest physical and mental shape that I had experienced throughout my MH education. Pat, later, told me that I smelled. I had showered and changed my underpants, before I came after a week of doing neither.

The ceremony started and a man of the cloth entered. I should've never known there were one-hundred-thirty-nine people behind me because, suddenly, I heard a pin drop. The serious man of faith spoke of Mom and her accomplishments. He spoke of her and of us; her immediate family. Next, Glenda stood up graciously. She moved to the lectern. She had on her serious PROX NEWS expression and used her serious tone of voice, as she delivered her prepared remarks. She said that Mom was an angel and that she was the best mother a person, like her, could have. Next, Lily spoke. She recapped how Mom struggled as she raised us alone. I never rose that day to speak. I never spoke a word, verbally, during the entire affair. Non-verbally, however, I spoke volumes. The casket was guided down the red carpet and rolled outside to the burial plot. The Religious Leader followed it, and we were behind them with our heads lowered.

The dreary day never went away. A cold rain fell and the wind was brisk. A large green tent housed the open six-foot deep grave with a mound of red earth adjoined to it. On the other side, six wooden folding chairs were reserved for the family. Glenda sat at one end. I sat at the other. Everybody looked somber. The uncomfortability level was high for the attendees. The cold temperature made the wind and rain even more wicked and unbearable. As people took shelter under the awning and beneath their umbrellas they all waited silently for the man of God to fall silent. The mound of earth had a silver spade in it. The funeral leader held out the spade and gestured for people to come forward and pay their respect. He shoved a spade with a symbolic amount of dirt into the hole; it was sent back to whence it came.

This was when, I think, *Mead* acted terribly.

Mindlessly, before a soul moved forward to take the tool, I popped out of my seat. I grabbed the shovel from the funeral leader's hand and briskly shoveled spade after spade full of red earth, back into its hole. The total amount that I transferred, five shovels full, covered her entire casket. I would have kept going, but someone tapped me on the shoulder to stop; which I did. I handed the spade to the person, and I returned to my seat avoiding eye contact with anyone.

The luncheon that followed brought everyone together again. Mom lived in a townhouse in a development. The downstairs was full of people. I walked upstairs and sat in an overstuffed chair. I was physically and mentally exhausted. I never knew it but *M*ead, at last, had broken me. I was present for those that gathered to mourn that day. But I never grieved, not even for a second. Plans were set in the late afternoon for dinner that evening. It was me, Uncle Stu, Glenda, Lily, Manuel, Pat and Frank. People came by day and night as we just sat there, on little chairs for seven-days. A mountain of food arrived. I answered the door once, and a neighbor brought us a lemon bundt cake. I hated lemon bundt cakes. But my eyes widened anyway as my dinky eyebrows raised in astonishment. I made an "ooh" sound to her. It was another one of my attempts to please someone. Because I was a people pleaser.

The meal that night consisted of an array of left overs from the luncheon earlier in the day. Afterwards it was Glenda's turn to take center stage. She pulled out the family photo albums and she went through each page. Lily got up and went into the kitchen as Glenda continued. She had a story for every photo. There was a black and white photo of me when I was seven. I had a huge booger coming out of my nose. Another one was of Mom. She stood in front of a clothes line filled with white sheets. Glenda pointed out that she was nine-months pregnant with me. And then she said: "Look at that serious expression on her face," and then she looked at me with sad puppy dog eyes. She acted gleeful and giddy as if she'd never seen some of them before.

Afterwards, Lily cleared the table; Pat helped her. Manuel sat in the living room and watched television as I listened to Uncle Stu and Glenda. They talked about Mom and they reminisced about people they once knew and who had died. They enjoyed their after meal coffee.

Maybe it was my fault. I asked Glenda where her boyfriend Pliartrum, Junior was. She looked at me like it's none of your fucking business. But it moved the ball into that territory. We argued. Our warm family expressions shifted to cold political stares. Everyone acted as if they were glued to their favorite news channels and they had just received word that their political foes crossed the line, again. But this time they went too far. Lily, who rinsed and loaded the dishwasher, stood in the doorway between the two rooms. She dried her hands with a dish towel.

She asked: "What in the hell is going on out here? Have you people lost your minds?"

Glenda took the bait. She offered her smart aleck expression as she filled our minds with the gut wrenching reports about the People Party. She stood for all the craziness. She had gobbledygook about toasters, banana cream pies, and *"I Love Lucy,"* who she described as a woman who brought no femininity to her role. "You could tell she didn't give a hoot about the way she looked and dressed. I thought that she was too drab." In her mind it was not " *I Love Lucy,"* it was: "Lesbians Love Lucy."

There was conflict everywhere. *M-watchers* relayed all of the data up the chain. Glenda declared war. Lilly's comments hit a homerun and Uncle Stu stared at her with contempt when the subject of religion arose.

Lily responded to Glenda's last utterance that God answered people's prayers. "So you think that God has the time to pay attention to every soul on the planet?" "And what about Jesus, Mohammed and Buddah," she asked.

Uncle Stu shot all of us down. He pointed his finger at Lily who had just sat back down. He said earnestly, "We're going to wipe you sons-of-bitches out."

If Uncle Stu had his way, Americans believed only in Pliartrum. The Rule of Law and democracy was denounced, and a new oligarchical system, similar to Russia, emerged. The entire Federal Government would be privatized. Even our militaries would be in private hands. They planned a purge. In their minds they've already swelled the ranks of Federal employees with "their people," but "there's more to be done," according to Glenda. "The takeover started on January 6, 2021, just ten-months ago." Pliartrum was out of Office by then. His War on America, however, went into action the second he left the nation's capital. He had people in place to monitor the internet, in particular, Youtube, for anything which was subversive to him. If there was something outrageous then the former president was made aware of it. That's how he saw Lily's comment. *Mead* had everyone beneath the sun under constant observation. *M-watchers* and m-workers maintained a tight grip as they controlled, and uncontrolled, the uncontrollable: mankind.

Chapter 20

I packed up my car, again, and I drove from Pennsylvania to California. I managed to settle all of my startup needs just like I always did; a studio apartment, a bed and recliner. Once again I unloaded the car. As I did it some men talked nearby. One said that he was a veteran. At that time I had the energy of a broken down lawn mower. I felt dragged down, as my possessions entered my latest dwelling. In and out I went until the conversation between the two men, I noticed, had stopped. Mindlessly, I approached the veteran and I told him that I was a veteran and that I was wondering where a veteran goes in the town to get help. He asked me: what kind of help? I said that I was sick. I was depressed.

That action had forethought. I was, once again, controlled by *Mead*. The *m-workers* had me on automatic pilot.

The veteran knew just what to do, since he had been mentally ill and homeless. The VA helped the Viet Nam vet. They paid his rent when he moved into his studio apartment. The next day a veteran's outreach worker met with me. Jack, the worker, was very tall and likable. After he came to my apartment that day I placed my dog in a dog-hotel, because once he interviewed me and completed his documentation, he drove me to Los Angeles. I spent two-weeks at a VA hospital in a locked MH unit. I was there voluntarily, but others were not. I had, of course, worked in one, but I had never been a patient in one. To me it made a difference. I felt comfortable there. But, I told nobody why. Days passed and I felt the depression lift. It was quite wonderful. I recuperated nicely. It took a year, but I dropped all of the excess weight, and most importantly, mentally; it was a new me. I was on an antidepressant, and cluster headaches left me alone for that year; I wondered, much later, why bBecause they came back when I began a new job in my old career. The new job required all *m-workers* to scramble, and it couldn't have been timed better, I realized later. This job required a physical and a drug test. I was in shape for both of them. There had been no marijuana in my system ever since I returned from the hospital a year ago. I had no need for it.

 I passed the tests and was hired. Later, I still took antidepressants. But the cluster headaches returned. When it happened it was bad. I knew just what to do. I obtained medical marijuana, it was before legalization, and I self-medicated. It battled the pain. I took a deep hit and I held it in as I thought: "Take that you mother fucker!" I could feel the battle going on. It was like a plumber's snake. It unclogged the congestion up the nostril. It took several hits until I turned the corner and it went away. Once, I was in Amsterdam, courtesy, of all people, Glenda. She had invited me, Frank and Lily to join her as she was on assignment in Paris. I went at her expense. The cluster headaches in France never relented. Once, she hired a tour bus. It took us to sights all over gay-paree. As the bus rolled by Parisians a cluster headache started. It got so bad it brought me to tears, which it had done before. I remembered that I looked right into Glenda's face, a foot from me, and I knew that my eye appeared as if it had been punched several times.

I screamed in agony: "YOU SEE!" She had no sympathy in her eyes because she hated me and she liked to see me suffer. Why was I invited? Because she always said that she loved me. Her actions told me otherwise.

I spent three-days in the city of canals. Its history never escaped me but I was there for the marijuana. Once purchased I bought a pipe. I went back to my hotel room and smoked. When I smoked, in those years, I always smoked a cigarette afterwards. I crushed the butt into an ashtray I laid down and I fell asleep. Hours later, however, I awakened with a terrible cluster attack. I grabbed the pipe and marijuana and went to the darkened bathroom. Any light agitated the pain even more and it was daytime. In the darkness I sat on the toilet seat. The pain roared like a lion that had been hit by a snap of the whip. My hands trembled as I stuffed the cannabis into the pipe. I shielded my tortured eye from the brightness of the flame. I deeply inhaled, something I couldn't do, if I didn't have a cluster headache, and I just wanted to get high. I held the medicine from God, and I sniffed it a few times to make the medicine go further up the nasal passage that was clogged.

On that day I experienced a miracle. The power of cannabis broke through the clog immediately. Woosh, it stopped. It took only seconds. That time I was freed from its grip on my brain and the dagger in my eye. To me it was a miracle. I stayed high while I was there. I walked through the city streets. Once, I stepped off a street curb. A few seconds went by before a quiet electric streetcar should've smacked right into me. I was in its path as I stepped onto the street. I wasn't injured or killed, and I believed if that was on the menu that day, it would have happened. Decades later I thanked *Mead* and the *m-team* for the marijuana experience that I had there. I was spared, that time, from the evil clutches of the suicide headache.

After that I used both psychotropics and cannabis. The job that I was hired for was in Sacramento. It was a non-profit organization. It had many treatment facilities located throughout the United States. I was hired into a new program; it started, only, a year ago. It was a day program for chronically mentally ill adults. The program required, though, a SMI diagnosis with psychosis. I was hired as a psychosocial rehabilitation specialist at a program called *Choices*. It was housed in an old MH unit of a psychiatric hospital that no longer existed. The rest of the building housed the county's social service offices. Our area had two padded seclusion rooms, which housed file cabinets. It also had a nurses station. It sat between eight rooms. They housed the patients in the old psych-ward. Now, those rooms were all offices. A secretary sat at the helm in the nurses station. The psychiatric nurse was also headquartered in that area. She was a woman born and bred in the country of Buddah, India. She always dressed in traditional Indian garments. She never wore anything else. We, also, had two social workers Sandy and Mark. There was a psychiatrist, Doctor Chavez, who came twice a week to see people. But the program had an odd executive director. His name was Bill. His oddity was that he was an administrator. He never led a MH program before. Besides that, frankly, he was weird. Once I walked a group into a group room. It was empty and we sat down and started the group. At least two-minutes went by and all of the sudden we heard the sound of a toilet in action; it flushed loudly. The sound came from the executive director's private bathroom. It seemed that we came in and started while he sat on the throne. He always reads the newspaper. I was aware of his routine because I cleaned and stocked each of the four bathrooms, that was my chore everyday, and his restroom was one of them. That day's print always side-saddled the commode. I knew because I threw it out Monday through Friday. After the group he called me to his office, and demanded to know why we were in there. I told him that I had no idea that he was in his restroom. The door to it was closed, and I didn't have a habit of knocking on it to check if he or anyone was in there. That's when I realized that he didn't like me. He hired me, so I was forever in his debt. He never harmed me in my eyes even though he tried…

I shared an office with another PSR worker, Ellen. She was very likable and giddy. We both ran separate psychosocial rehabilitation groups twice per day. For the rest of our time we provided case management services. Just like I did when I was a psychiatric caseworker. People, especially those with chronic mental illness, had a lot of case management needs, and I did my best. I performed one good deed after another. In fact, I performed so many good deeds during my MH education, that I felt, years later, it offset my teenage criminality, which would have surely continued if *Mead* had not pulled the plug on it.

On average twenty SMI people from the community spent their day with us. Some were homeless and came to us by day, and by night they went back to the shelters. Others came to us as referrals. They lived all over the county, and one of my jobs was to transport people. We rarely picked anybody up, but we routinely drove them home in a fifteen-passenger van after the program closed for the day. Of all of the positions that I served, in so many other capacities in the field, this assignment was the best because I was filled with knowledge. Thoughts presented themselves to me at all hours of the day and night. I wrote down each one on scratch paper. Everyday, there was more. I kept them in a big plastic bag. Prior to my employment I wrote a book. I used the knowledge in the book and at the new job. The words that I offered were not mine. I never took credit for another's work, which Bill did to me once… but, frankly, I never knew where it came from. I never read anything about it. I never watched or listened to anything either. And, I never talked about it with anyone. I, honestly, never knew of *Mead* in those days. I worked in the right orbit, but I never tuned into *Mead*. Nobody did. It tuned into me for some reason. Through all of those years, I never processed my criminality, even though I was well aware of it. Having an awareness that something was wrong. It still bothered me a great deal, because I wanted to know? What does all this mean? And, why was I blinded by *Mead*, for half a century, until the knowledge was revealed, and then processed? I never knew exactly what occurred. It was quite remarkable because my whole being lived and worked in a MH arena. It stayed with me every hour that I remained awake. The answers, to my questions, were right in front of me the whole time. I knew the different diagnostic terms. SMI people were diagnosed with this in the process of my work. But I never held a clinical position, and, so, I never knew the symptoms for being diagnosed with Bipolar. Or I never knew about personality disorders symptoms of things like schizoid personality disorder (SPD) or antisocial personality disorder (ASPD).\. I knew the headlines of diagnosis i.e. schizophrenia, but, never once, in all of my years of service did I just open a book to read about what the criteria was for that diagnosis. I never bothered to look. I had no need to. It wasn't part of my work. Why people were diagnosed with it was none of my business. I had a job, and I did it. As for me, I saw a psychiatrist at the VA, and I was on antidepressants. It wasn't until my twilight years that it was finally revealed to me. *Mead* gave me a taste of myself, again. I was deceived for decades… If I knew the truth, at any time, my MH career would've ended. Because, I learned later, that I hadn't even come out of the womb, and I was already damned…

I wanted to know who I actually was. The competent MH employee, the substitute teacher, the MH client, the patient, or the thief? Why was I the way I was? I cried loneliness, but it was not that. I just wanted to befriend people for two things – sex and marijuana. If people I knew weren't in either category, I would be friendly. I helped them if I could. But I never connected socially. I never spent time with regular people, especially after work. I went home to my little dog back then, and I stayed alone. Six-and-one-half decades went by before the puzzle, finally and fully, presented itself. I must put it together. I solved it, over a period of time, but really, it did not take very long…

I recalled strong memories. A single moment, forty-five years ago, still burned brightly inside of me, just like they all did. The romantic couple on the television flashed me back to when I stood on an escalator going up. I was in a department store, and I looked up in front of me and there was a heterosexual couple. They held hands. The strong visual memory was always accompanied by equally strong audio. It was an old *Moody Blues* song. The tune and a single lyric played in my mind…: *Gazing at people, some hand-in-hand, just what I'm going through they can't understand…*

But, I did, and it changed things for me.

No longer was my MH education just about the good side. A flow of wisdom warmed my eyes. It came one piece at a time. I compiled the pieces, and along with my good side, shtick, and the psychosocial rehabilitation information it turned out good. I was successful in the short run. SMI people smiled, and some told me that they liked being at the program. Some, I recalled, told me that they felt good when they were there. Folks got involved in the groups. Attitudes were positive. People were genuinely kind. The seeded information led to one thing: the growth of goodness.

The leadership of the program, including the psychiatrist, wanted to know what I was doing. They interviewed clients.

They asked them what they've learned in my group. They wanted to see some of the hand-out materials. They questioned my work. None of the leadership ever sat in one of my groups, which they were welcomed to do. But when Bill found out what I taught he just told me that I had to stop using acronyms. That was it. They didn't question me about the content of the philosophy. If they did I would have told them; it was knowledge passed down to me, for me to pass on to others.

But it wasn't all roses. I had my critics. I recalled there were two program members who stopped coming to my group in my second year. They were, usually, at the program for the entire day, but they never came into my groups anymore. One of them said that I talked too much. That he hardly ever got time to say anything. I explained that I taught behavioral skills. It wasn't a free-for-all discussion group. It was structured, well, sort of. My bag of notes came out. There must have been a hundred little notes. I reached in and pulled a few out, and whatever topic the notes covered, I used them along with everything else during the therapeutic hour. However, because I was a people pleaser. I accepted the criticism from the two, and I made changes. I still taught behavioral skills, but I shortened my presentations. It opened discussion for the last fifteen-minutes of the hour. Those two guys never showed up, regardless.

The county started a new housing development for the homeless. To those who met the criteria it meant they received a new, one-bedroom, apartment. It was stocked with everything: The furniture, plates, silverware, glasses, a coffee maker, sheets, pillow cases, cleaning supplies, even toilet paper. Two clients in our program met the criteria. Applications were completed, and I helped one of them as he moved into his new home. Bill loved the story. The company had a monthly newsletter. He decided that he wanted me to take photographs of one of them at his new home. He, also, wanted me to write a story about it. He planned to send it to the company's newsletter for publication. So, I did it. Weeks went by and one day, the new newsletter was issued. On the front page of it was one of the pictures that I took that day. Along with it was my story. Every word of it made it into ink, except who wrote it. My name was omitted and Bill's name replaced it. Bill sent an email to each of us; it stated that I deserved all the credit.

Soon, Mead, I later learned, ordered another transition after two years at that job. This time instead of me having another crisis; it was Dad instead. His last one. I was on medical family sick-leave for six-weeks. I stayed at his place and I visited him for a few hours everyday. I realized, much later, that I was, finally, being processed out of the MH field. *Mead* played with me first. I was sent through hell to get to where I felt safe, happy and secure. Meanwhile, the desire to find other MH jobs entered my consciousness. I thought about going back to work for the State. I completed an application. I drove eight-hours round trip to the interview. They liked what I said, but, when all was said and done, they never hired me. Someone in State personnel got wind that I applied, once again, for a MH position with the State. My last "I quit" departure caused the word to get out: State jobs were closed to me.

Soon after, Dad called me. He needed my help. He was not well, and he lived five-hours away, and because, at age eighty, he was my father, I used sick leave and went to him. The hospital hooked him to a machine for six-weeks, and the day his insurance ran out they shipped him to a hospice. He died alone; I didn't know that he was shipped. *Mead* spared me from going to his funeral. When I went back to California, my energy was drained. I couldn't drive five-hours or five-minutes. Dad's sister, a great aunt, Frank and Pat all came from the east coast... They held a little ceremony for him at the Veterans' cemetery, where his ashes were interred.

If *Mead* ever shared any secrets it was now. It was a crazy path. When I returned from Dad's ordeal, Bill was super pissed at me. He, actually, wrote me up for taking off for six-weeks, and said, "I never called in." He knew, when I left, that I took family sick leave so that I could be with my Dad. Besides, I gave him the paperwork the doctor signed; he approved my absence. But, Bill went ahead with the admonishment anyway. I let him write me up. I never questioned him. Like I said, he could do no harm. He changed his tune, later, that day. I understood. He shifted to an "aw, shucks" attitude. I thought it was because the company's personnel director told him what he did was a violation of the law, ergo, he discriminated against me, and I could have initiated a civil-rights complaint with the federal Civil Rights Division. I believed that I would have won. But, I never did anything. Even so, I was out-the-door two-weeks after I returned to California.

Mead had the *m-team* in action. *It* instructed *m-watchers* to ensure my quick departure, just as before in the navy... *M-workers* used a staff meeting. *It* delivered the means necessary for Bill to escort me off the property, because I was fired, on the spot. *Mead* knows my weaknesses. *M-planners* were familiar and knew what was deep inside of me. What I expected. It had been years since I had sex. I gave up all of my attempts at socializing. I was never in a position to possibly have a sexual experience. At a lull in the staff meeting Ellen told me that one of the clients, and she named him, "really likes you." There were no more words. But, it didn't matter. *Mead* triggered it. The revelation led me into action. The day before I was fired, I took people home from the program. I planned that the client and myself were the last two in the van. *M-workers* shot a gush of sexual desire in me. I told the client, who liked me, that I had strong feelings for him. A power overwhelmed me with feelings that I never had before. He told me had that same feeling. He came up front. It was really strange because I had never, in all of my MH years, told a client that, or looked for sexual or personal relationships with anyone that I served. He gave me a kiss on the cheek when I dropped him off. Of course, I later realized what I did was a complete violation of the rules. But, I was blinded to the consequences. We never got to the sex part because I came to work the next day, and I conducted my morning group. There were new program participants, they were first timers, so I presented the big picture.

Basically, my information, from *Mead*, was about self. Understanding the soul and self. We talked about the importance of having: Self-awareness, self respect, self esteem, self confidence and self kindness. That was called ARECK. Then there was RFGLUCK, which stood for: Respect, friendship, goodness, love, understanding, compassion and kindness; towards self and others. I presented information about how the self and soul must be "united." I asked them to recall a saying, which stemmed from World War I. "United We Stand, Divided We Fall." I emphasized how critical and important it was to show respect for our vehicle of life. I emphasized self because I understood that people with mental illness, especially, serious mental illness, cared very little for themselves. I wanted to introduce them to themselves. We always heard of people who've said: "I need to find myself." I said: well, today, you found it. Treated as you would want others to treat you. I presented my shtick about the difference between our good-side and our bad-side. With self, the way I put it: The soul and self come together to create a person. And, after our journey through life, self was buried in the ground, and soul returned from whence it came.

It was to be my final performance. At the end of the group one new group participant popped out of his seat. He approached me and stuck out his hand. I remembered he said: "That was great." I was always touched when those kinds of moments happened, and it helped, in particular, on what was to be, otherwise a gloomy day.

So, I was out of job. Later, I realized all of these events were courtesy of *Mead*. I left California and moved in with Ellen, in Las Vegas. I had money to support myself for at least six-months, I told her. I attempted to return to the non-profits in the MH field. I drove a six-hour round trip back to California. I interviewed in front of three people. Everything went fine until we got into specifics. I talked about my experience. I spoke about the types of behaviors and how I handled certain matters. The questioner asked me something like: "What would you do if you had a group of chronically mentally ill adults who had no coping skills?

I spoke about what I did, and everything was going fine up to that point. At the conclusion of my answer I spoke about how people felt better about themself and were more relaxed with themselves and with others, which was the feedback I received. As I ended my answer, I sat back and casually said: "Then I watch all of the magic begin."

The two other panelists never looked up at me until I said that, they were writing the whole time. The questioner asked: "What magic is that?" I just answered it's the magic that occurred when people liked themselves better. When they opened up and actually lived. He patted me on the back and put his arm around my shoulder as we walked out of the office. I was never hired. I went back to Las Vegas, and after the money ran out, I applied for Social Security Disability. I never worked in the MH field again. For thirty-years I was on the job day and night. I worked with client after client. I served patient after patient. I was still tortured by cluster headache after cluster headache. Delirium now seemed to have struck me. I was the ball and it was the baseball bat. Awakened each night, as I slept. I deduced, much later, that my MH education, from *Mead*, had been completed. *Mead* insisted, however, that I held on to something for the decades to come.

Chapter 21

From what I learned and read Lily's demise was thoroughly investigated by the city's police. The detective in charge was Kaz Jackson. He was like a vicious guard dog, once he sunk his teeth in, he never let go. Officially, the crime remained unsolved. But, in reality, he learned to take heed of his first hunch, because in the first few minutes of an investigation, he was spot-on a lot of the time. It was true a *911* call had been initiated by Manuel, at three-fifteen a.m., and that Lily lay dead, in her bed, with an ax wedged into the back of her skull. How, exactly, the ax got there was still in question. At an interrogation conducted hours later, Manuel presented the day's events in a cogent manner. There was no physical evidence. He had not been arrested. In a report the detective wrote: "There were no scratches, bruises, cuts or any sign of blood visible to the naked eye on his person."

From what I gathered, Manuel talked a smart game but his articulated words only deceived.. To Detective Jackson, the minor was a possible suspect in his mother's murder. The young man, however, reported that he heard nothing that night because his room was on the other end of the house from hers. At an interrogation he claimed that he slept through the hours the coroner had determined, as to, the time of his adopted mother's expiration. Jackson sized up the individual that he had in front of him. He determined that Manuel deceived him when asked how he knew that his mother was dead if he heard nothing that night, because he lived, as he claimed, on the other side of the house. But, he let it go, for the moment, because he had no other evidence to arrest him on.

At the same time the police now had Lily's computer. But the contents only threw a monkey wrench into the fresh investigation. The detective had evidence, which connected President Pliartrum to Lily. He found a folder filled with emails between her and friends, and more importantly, emails sent to different newspapers. She wrote in her cover letters that her comment and Pliartrum's post, just hours later, were linked. She felt it revealed a lot about the ousted leader. Linkage made it clear, she wrote, because it punched him again and again. It hit home. Right where it really hurt. But, she added, in her emails, that she never wrote the comment to him. She offered her opinion of the video. Her comment was about Pliartrum's criminality and, if found guilty, his imprisonment.

"Pliartrum's record was clear. If you punched him he punched back. And, since the murdered woman was an unknown civilian; I wouldn't put it past him to do more than punch her back; he could have ordered her demise."

The D.A. moved his hands to the top of his head and leaned back in his seat. "I'm listening," he said to Kaz. "Pliartrum's words on Jewish Americans, and the fact that her comment never mentions religion. But her userID was her name; it told us that she was Jewish." The lawman said that the former president's post was about Israel and American Jews. To him the "boss" issued a veiled threat to Lily when Pliartrum said in his last sentence; "*before it is too late!*" Jackson pegged it for further investigation, I learned much later.

On the morning of Lily's funeral I picked Pat up. Frank went to work in the morning, and he told her that he'd meet us at the Funeral. Pat looked bad. Alcohol and Pliartrum's addictive drug had scoured her beauty which once was. A kind and generous person, all of her life, she looked downtrodden and needy, because her son awaited justice.

But, who wanted to murder such a defenseless person in such a brutal fashion. I never believed or imagined that it was her own son who stood, solemnly, at the helm of his late mother's grief. I looked at him that day. He was in the spotlight. He delivered a great performance, that is, if he was the guilty party. He was smooth. Very smooth. I wondered, when he spoke, "did he twist the truth to fit his needs? Had he deceived all of us? Like a pro, I thought."

More than three-hundred people turned out from the community where Lily was very well known, primarily due to her pottery school and her politics. Manuel remained somber throughout but he was to profit from her murder to the tune of one-hundred-thousand dollars. I knew he felt good about that. I ravaged for several seconds. Suddenly, I pictured Lily's sweet eyes. They glowed. I felt her spirit. But, then, I saw her expression. It was filled with horror. Her eyes sunken by dread. Her anguished being cried out: "Why?" "She was asleep at the time it happened," Detective Jackson told me.

The news of Lily's murder spreaded like a wildfire. I understood it. Her expiration date arrived. But why in such horrific fashion. Evil did her in, because whoever drove an ax into the back of her skull came from a "depraved and savaged hereditary," according to the Detective. His team had the murder weapon. The object, lodged in her skull, was removed, carefully, by the coroner. Its long wooden handle caught the fingerprints of both the victim and her son because the murder weapon came from the garage. It was regularly used, according to Manuel; "we alternated and chopped wood for the fireplace, often." They even had a stone; it sharpened the tool.

I rolled my eyes when I saw Uncle Stu and Glenda that day. They arrived in her chauffeured limousine. He wore a tuxedo, black-framed, round-lensed glasses, with a black derby atop his gray head. Glenda wore a conservative black dress and shoes along with a light black veil. It matched her heart, I thought. When she came to Mom's funeral she wore her everyday business attire. But that day, the murder in our family became sensational nationwide news. It was reported on by every cable news network. PROX NEWS had three Country Club Party political pundits, who discussed the matter, on the second highest rated show behind GLenda's.

"Society crumbles and things like this happen because of the evil People Party," one proclaimed. "People like Lily don't own guns," the other said, "they're just like sitting ducks."

The political voices went on to say that they predicted major civil unrest; disruptions in gas, water and electricity. "Stores will have empty shelves," one relished, "The nation's supply lines will be cut." And, the know-it-alls never let a minute go-by without his name being mentioned. "I think that this nation's real president; President Plairtum, will have these matters under control. Nothing like it ever happened when he's in Office. There will be no interruptions. Public safety is assured. So, when he is back in his rightful spot, you'll be rest assured. But, if he doesn't win a second time, well, there's no doubt; the election was stolen because it was rigged." "And besides that," I thought, "he'd only keep running for Office, until he, finally, won his second term."

The layout of the cemetery added Mom, almost a year ago. Now, along with Mom-Mom and Pop-Pop, it was Lily who entered its grounds. They placed her next to Mom. A sadness emerged, which was rare for me. I felt a lot of emotion when my dog Rusty expired. And, I had a sense of sadness when my grandparents had all expired too. But it wasn't painful. I clearly remembered how I felt then: vacant. Inside of me, however, the emptiness, which I experienced when Mom and then Dad expired, was gone. I felt the loss of Lily, and I watched her son, Manuel, on that day, he looked like he lost his best friend. A city council woman read the eulogy as hearts sank deeper and deeper.

On that day, it didn't, but the basement had acted as the post funeral location for the grieved. For decades, Pat's family came together there. When Pat's Mom and Dad died everybody was there. Not for Lily. It never happened. Mom-Mom said, years ago, that Glenda told Mom that she would never step inside of Frank's home again. She labeled it as a germ-fest and a hazard zone. Uncle Stu wanted everyone to gather in the presidential suite that he occupied at the nicest hotel in the city. I walked through its gilded entryway past the Norwegian Guard dressed in full attire. I looked around at all the gaudiness; I wanted to puke. There was a private elevator: it transported someone, only after security checks and verification of invitation. That took a while because no-one was there to approve of me. The hotel concierge suggested a comfortable chair for me to sit in while I waited.

 I sat for twenty-minutes. I saw people of material wealth; it's written all over some of their plastic surgery. I thought. The cost of the luggage that rolled by me could feed a village in Africa, I thought. I looked at my phone as my peripheral eyesight caught Uncle Stu as he entered through the expensive entryway. With both hands he carried a cake sized box. He approached the chair and I stood up. "Hey, booby;" a name he gave me in childhood. He always used it whenever I was in his presence. "I always feel sympathetic when I'm with you," he said. "Because people like you", he quipped, "never get the taste of the good life." I didn't disagree because I ate mostly processed food. I never recalled, as an adult, when I ever ate a well-balanced meal, other than, in the navy, or at a homeless shelter.

I stood up and we walked to the private elevator. Before we turned the corner he stopped in his tracks. He sighed and said: "Will you hold this?" He extended his arms for me to take the cake box. "I can't let the butler see me doing anything that he should be doing. He's very sensitive. He sees himself as my puppet without strings."

"Well," I told Uncle Stu with conviction, "I don't get high on money. I'm not sure why. But I think you played a role in that, huh, Uncle Stu. Did you teach me about doing something good with money, or to do what was selfish, greedy and, frankly, immoral; it was very unhealthy to my development." I held out my arms and handed him the cake box. He took it with his mouth open. As I stepped into the gilded private elevator, which took me thirty-two floors up to the suite; Uncle Stu followed me. Stupid or antagonistic I said something smart ass about the former "crime boss." And, then he lectured me on my support of Lily's politics, and he denounced Lily's advocacy against Pliartrum.

I remembered that I swallowed hard, but I told him that "Pliartrum was responsible for two plagues on this nation, his covid response and his presidency. The ladder of which we won't recover from for generations to come. If ever." And when he said that people like me and Lily, don't really care about the country, because if we did, we'd come to our senses and support Pliartrum and his vision. I thought he should've warned me that he had a German chocolate cake inside of the box he held, because I love German chocolate cake.

I told him that Pliartrum was a crook. He skipped a beat, and then he said, "I wish you all the best. Good luck." When the golden doors opened, on the way out, I tripped him as he exited the lift. They both flew forward. The cake flew the furthest. It spilled out onto the privileged carpet that was an inch thick. My uncle, on the floor, looked back at me with bloody murder in his eyes. I hit the elevator button hard, and as the doors closed; his butler tended to him.

Chapter 22

Boris was locked away in a juvenile detention facility for nine-months before he saw a lawyer. He spent a great deal of his time locked away from others. He was alone for two reasons: One, for his own safety due to the sensational crime he inflicted on the poor old woman, and on the community. Two, his ASPD was chronic. He couldn't be in the company of others because of his explosive personality.

I believed that Boris was never exposed to his goodness. Most folks have, at least, one drop of it inside of them; however, for Boris, it was never placed on his plate. It wasn't even on the menu, therefore, he never experienced people who modeled and communicated their goodness through their facial expressions, tone and manner. I talked to Boris, years ago, when I visited Frank, and he was a young child. My appearances in his life only occurred when I "traveled," and I wasn't, exactly, in good condition. In fact, I was in very poor condition when he saw me as he grew up. I stayed with Frank and Pat for a couple of weeks when the boy was fourteen-years old.

As I sat across from him. I told him that poor parenting didn't mean he can't do what's right now..

I saw Boris as a caged animal inside his own mind, most everyone snapped a whip at him. Boris was the flip side of the people pleaser. Every soul he encountered he sought hatred from them. He wanted people to hate him. Everyone was repulsed by him. He repulsed himself, he told me, in an email. I offered to correspond with him because I knew that the boy didn't, like, come out of the gate right, like a thoroughbred.

When I visited Boris, I sat in the waiting room for a few minutes before he came out. I looked around the facility, and at the faces that I saw. They all looked pained. Later, I told the junior convict: not everybody knew how to parent when they have a kid. I explained that his mother and father were young, mindless. They never counted on you. It just happened like that, sometimes, I told him. They treated you like you weren't even there, sometimes. But they treated you just like they were treated.

Boris replied: "Did your dad ever use a padlock to lock you in your room?"

Before the murder his mind was locked into a delusion that he was a superstar in the video game world. He never set it as a goal. He acted it out in his mind, regularly I learned. He acted like he made it. That he was already there. The boy said: "It's all sewn up; it's all going to happen." What was sewn up was his future. He was tried as an adult for first-degree murder in State Court. Boris was just like thousands of other young men. They're walking timebombs.

Boris faced a determined prosecutor who sought the maximum sentence: death. "The elder he slaughtered required the harshest penalty," said the prosecutor, William Carter told the judge.

The lady of great age was just like Lily, and didn't deserve her fate. The crimes against them belonged only in a Hollywood Script. Boris sought no notoriety, but he got a lot of it, nonetheless. The press poured into the area. Internet Youtube went wild; there were three-different channels which covered everything; sometimes, too much. Pundits projected their strong opinions, as usual. One described

Boris as the twenty-first-Century's poster child for "creepy murderers." The court was besieged by the media. The sensationalism of Glenda, the queen of PROX NEWS, possibly, having a nephew on death row, made tabloid headlines. Anything that Glenda did, provocatively, was covered in the rags. They had news teams at the courthouse from different networks. Police presence was beefed up. Add Boris and his crime into the mix, and PROX NEWS competitors, were like a bumble-bee on a flower. It buzzed and pollinated, profusely.

Chapter 23

The thrill ride that I "traveled" had so many inclines, dips and curves that I learned, but I was still blinded and I had no insight. I never readied myself for anything; how could I? There were so many things to prepare, and I never knew what was going on. I possessed knowledge and significant lessons. I understood, later, that I absorbed them consciously and subconsciously. Some were simple, which I acted upon. Some I was blinded to by *Mead*. I was never ready. I wallowed in my troubles. *M-workers* bit me with, mind crippling, cluster headaches and despair. Insight was impossible.

When Bill escorted me out of the building, I felt no shame. I was not embarrassed. I didn't mind it at all. It never fazed me. And, it wasn't until later, that I learned the reason why. It was all *Mead*, and the *m-team.* I was rescued so many times, but I never wondered and I never asked myself: Why? I never questioned the speed at which I was removed from angst. I was, of course, aware of it, but I never asked myself or wondered. Why was I always relieved from trouble or danger? I always felt lucky, later, when it happened. When I looked back it still amazed me the way it all unfolded. I was happy it happened, and it should have amazed me. It didn't because I never thought about it. I never reflected on anything in those years. I was relieved each time, hence, I never sought insight. I never figured out what it was all about. I only did that, if there was a problem. When something was wrong; and I needed answers. Only then did I ask myself. Otherwise, my blindness continued unabated.

The years that followed amazed me even more. I was down and the referee stood over me with his countdown to my demise. I was, I thought, history. But my depression always led me back to the VA, and since I had no income, I received free medical benefits. I saw a psychologist once a month. I was on psychotropics, which were prescribed by my psychiatrist, Doctor Wesson, who I saw every six-months. For three years, I paddled water. My Social Security Disability application was denied twice. The third time, it required that I appeared before a Social Security Judge… But, in the meantime, something happened. It changed my future.

I was surprised. However, at the same time it was right in front of my senses for thirty-years. Once again, I failed. I made no progress. I still wasn't ready. I remained blind. No access was granted; these mysteries all just piled up inside of me. Soon, it happened. Insight was generated. I thought, facetiously, that it was all piled up. Crap in my mind, And it was brought on by all the pressure in my brain from the cluster headaches. Seriously, the insight, slowly, dripped into me; its wisdom was absorbed by my coffer. A lot of my questions were answered but not all… I heard the diagnostic term before, so a lot of it, quickly, fit into place.

One day, I was at the VA. My monthly appointments continued for three-years with my psychologist. Frankly, though, I spun my wheels the entire time. I held onto my history of criminality. I never disclosed it to him or anyone, ever. When I finished my monthly appointment with him,

Doctor Wesson caught me as I left the psychologist's office. "I want to set a diagnostic appointment with you."

I heard the term before. I knew it was the longest appointment that one could have with a psychiatrist. It went on for two-hours. Every answer that I provided she entered into her computer. Her questions focused on my history. I told her how I picked up and "traveled," but I omitted my crazy teenage escapades. I remembered clearly that she gazed out on me for a second when I spoke of the times that I "traveled." She froze and softly uttered: "*guilty*." I saw that it clicked in her mind when she said it to herself. I watched her, for that nick of time, as she reacted, queerly, to her own observation.

She asked: "Have you ever had a period in your life where you felt really good, and you slept very little but you had a lot of energy?

I told her what I experienced. I recalled the wonderment of it all. "I felt so fantastic," I told her, "it lasted for weeks," I added. She stopped typing, looked up at me and said: "You're bipolar." I knew dozens of people with that diagnosis. I knew that it was a mood disorder, but I never knew any specifics. When, finally, I learned of the behaviors that led to a diagnosis; it hit me like an anvil. How stupid could I be to miss something as important as that. Or, was it that I, simply, was blinded, for all of those years… It was right in front of me the whole time. There was no other explanation.

Once I knew about my bipolar I processed a lot of my past. Some things started to make sense to me. I acknowledged insight, and I scribbled notes on scratch paper as to why I was the way I was. Ever since I was attached to the VA system, I was encouraged to do something about it like counseling, groups and medication. Nothing was out of bounds. So I sought financial relief from the VA, because of the sexual assaults fifty years ago. I was diagnosed with PTSD and I sought service-connected disability compensation. In my claim, I explained what happened a half-century ago, and how it had impacted my adult life. I wrote about my social isolation. I relayed my lack of friends. I admitted that I never sought romance. I spoke of the nightmares and flashbacks, but, what also ate at me was the family aspect to all of this. Oh, how those wounds were so raw and exposed. It stayed that way for another decade...

In the meantime, I had applied for Social Security Disability. I got a date for a hearing before a judge. Immediately, I reached out because when a person went before a Social Security Judge, they needed representation. I knew it from experience. As a case manager I accompanied clients to their hearings; they all had representation.
Johnson, Brick and Meaker, Attorneys-at-Law, was the number one, Social Security disability, law office in town. I understood what took place, and I shuddered at the thought of one. I never wanted an attorney, they took a big chunk if you won your case. But, reality set in and I called them. Kathy Swabb, was an attorney-assistant. She had a secretary, which was who I spoke with initially. The actual lawyers, themselves, never got involved with anything. The secretary wanted to know specific information: One, the nature of my disability, and two, my social media account information. I told her that I had more than one disability. I was diagnosed with PTSD, Bipolar and cluster headaches. I also told her that I had a noncancerous brain tumor, according to an MRI. I told her that I was not on social media, and I never had been. I awaited a decision as to representation. The secretary called me the next day. She told me that my case was accepted. My hearing was six-months away. I was able to get by, only, because of Ellen. When I arrived I paid her for more than a year until my money ran out. I sought and received food stamps, and Ellen

patiently waited three-years for my Social Security Disability decision.

It wasn't easy. The press followed and reported on President Pliartrum's crackdown on all kinds of benefits for poor people who utilize the resources of the Federal Government's safety-net. People on Social Security Disability became an obsession with him. Some judges had their hands tied. They were forced to deny based on stricter criteria. Others, reportedly, reveled in their cruelty to dismiss what an applicant claimed. The process itself was very dysfunctional. Months later her secretary called and set up an appointment for me. I met with Kathy, and we discussed the hearing and my case. In ten-days, I appeared before the judge. My pre-court meeting, with Kathy, didn't go well. I felt uncomfortable and defensive as she asked me questions. She pushed my buttons that day, and I left with a soggy feeling as if I peed my pants. Three days and a week passed. I entered the Federal Building, and I cleared security. I entered the outer offices of the two courtrooms, and I took a seat. When Kathy arrived she said something about the judge. I side-stepped it and I told her: "You pushed my buttons the other day." She looked at me and said: "I was only asking you questions that the judge will ask." I replied: "Well, it's not going to happen today." I was super serious. I felt no nerves. I did not fear the judge, as if I was the *Cowardly Lion* and I stood before *The Wizard of Oz*.

My name was called. When I went through the door into the courtroom, immediately, my eyes met the man's eyes who was raised above me. We were, at least, ten-yards away but when our eyes linked, the overseer of Social Security Disability, Judge Willam C. Taylor was taken aback. My Attorney's Assistant sat at one table; I was at another. After I sat down, my dead serious feelings and expressions sat with me. I looked up at the Judge again. Once again, he was taken aback. I registered each non-verbal communication into my central nervous system. He questioned me first about an issue that I never raised in my disability application.. He said: "The first disability you claim is your thyroid."

I was shocked: "I never put that down as one of my disabling conditions! It's true, I do not have a thyroid anymore, it was radiated, and I take a little pill in the morning, which gives me my thyroid hormone. That's it. "It is not a disability," I told him. The hearing continued. He asked a number of questions that I gave precise answers to. Some of the questions were things like. "Do you care for a pet?"
"No," I replied.
"How did you get to the hearing today?"
"By car, I was dropped off." I never explained much about my disabilities. All of my medical records information was in front of him in black and white.
He asked me: "How many cluster headaches did you have last month."
I never hesitated and said: "Three." I wished I could have told him how many hit me, before I had a steady supply of cannabis. Then I would have answered: "More than thirty!" But, of course, I never talked about it because it was illegal to use cannabis back then; even for medical purposes. The hearing went on for twenty-minutes. *Mead* decided to make an appearance on my behalf. It took control of me. I never knew of *Mead* then. Suddenly, out of nowhere, in the middle of my hearing, my right arm slowly reached out and it rose to my eye level. My hand clenched. I looked at my fist a foot away from my face and, through my lips. *Mead* bellowed four-words: **_"I WILL NOT SUICIDE."_** My arm lowered and I never flinched. I knew that I never raised my arm. I never clenched my fist. And, the words were not mine. They came from my being, but I never initiated them. Without doubt it was *Mead*, and the reason that I, later, was so sure about that was because it was so obvious to me what happened. I retrospected a lot about all of those crazy years. I added

everything up. My accounting was ongoing though… Gradually, I understood, and I was given full access to me. What I found was that *Mead* had dealt with me ever since I was a child. I was mischievous even back then. Later, I understood that *it* dealt with everybody. It took me a long time until I got the answer that I searched for. What's really going on…?

At the conclusion of the hearing the judge looked at me and said: "I think I can make a decision on your case." I rose, my poker demeanor lasted even after I left his courtroom. I met Kathy at the door. She said to me: "He can't deny this one." Out in the waiting area, Kathy told me that I did good, and then she took me to her office and gave me a bottle of water. I downed it. Ellen picked me up that day. Three-weeks later, the Judge's decision came down. In the era of "disability scams," as Pliartrum put it. The honorable servant of the Courts ruled in my favor. I was given three-years worth of benefits. I paid Ellen off, and after that I gave her three-hundred dollars a month for rent. In the meantime, *m-planners, m-developers and m-coordinators* went over all the data, determined the facts, and made recommendations to *Mead* as to my disposition and future. This was all in retrospect, of course. My mind collated, finally. In the meantime, I was out of action. *Mead* physically disabled me for two months, decades ago. I never did anything. I, simply, picked up a thirteen-inch television off the ground. It weighed only five-pounds. Instantly, I was damaged. Frozen, I simply absorbed life events. No insight. I went from one pot of boiled water to another. I had more *Mead* episodes inside of me than *The Simpsons*. I possessed pieces of the puzzle, but there were still some that I needed. They were important pieces, too, I thought, but I still had no clue. *Mead* ordered the *m-team* that I was due for a major shift in my life. However, *they* were instructed to make the shift difficult… At that point my life was in limbo.

I still lived with Ellen, but I still "traveled." I looked, in earnest, for housing along the Washington coast. I came across an ideal housing opportunity. A veteran, John, who was gay, lived alone on a private island off the Washington coast. He posted an ad, which I came across as I searched the Internet. He offered to rent a room in his home. The rent was affordable, I had a monthly check from Social Security. I emailed him and inquired about it. He wrote back that he had a tenant right now, but he planned to move out next month.

Years later, I realized how *Mead* had shifted my tectonic plates. I never drove across the country again. For four-decades I had been on the road in between MH assignments from *Mead*. The word came down. M-*workers* were ordered by the *m-watchers*. This time, it should have been no different. The *m-team* reported to *Mead* that I was finished with my mental health education. It was time I faced up to other sore spots of my being...

When I "traveled," I went, practically, everywhere in the continental US, except for States like Washington; it was too far north. This time, however, I planned to go there. I still wanted things: I wanted a friend. I wanted a relationship; I still dreamt and hoped.. I never understood why I never had those human experiences. I just had a lot of sex. There was never any love. Oh, I fretted about the lack of friendship and love in my life to psychologists and myself. But then I left his office or turned on the television, and I accepted the solitude. I was, really, fine being alone. Some folks hated solitude. I knew that I was not one of those. But, society and Barbara Striesand said to me as I grew that "people who need people, are the luckiest people in the World." I wanted luck. I believed I should've made friends. I felt I should've had a relationship. Why I missed out on all of these basic human functions remained clouded.

A month went by and John wrote me an email. He told me that the room was vacant. He said that he needed somebody to take him into Seattle, for shoulder replacement surgery. He was inpatient for two-days. I took care of his dog and picked him up after his hospitalization. It took a two-hour drive, both ways.

I never figured this guy out until I got there. I had no vehicle, but I needed to take a supply of cannabis with me, as well as my dog, Pearl. No airplanes. I rented a car in Las Vegas. I drove to the location sixty-miles west of Tacoma; it was about one-thousand miles. The human and the canine took a ferry, which made trips between the island and the mainland.

I never had anything but sexual relations with people my age. No relationships. Men and women have laid beside me but no one ever loved me, and, more importantly, I never loved anyone else. It bothered me at times. This time, however, I arrived at his very nice, two-story home. It, and other homes, sat on an island, which was one-mile long.

He had one thing in mind the minute I arrived. He took me by the arm to the bedroom. He took off his clothes. I shrugged and followed his lead. We laid together, naked, on his king-sized bed. Nothing sexual happened, however. I never got it up. Either *Mead* kept it down without my knowledge… Or, I simply wasn't attracted to him. I never understood; it never happened before. I took him into Seattle to the VA Medical Center; I dropped him off. I went back to the island via ferry, and I cared for his dog and mine.

After the Social Security decision I wanted a dog just like Rusty. She came to me through the internet. She was the most beautiful mutt that I ever saw. The *m-team*, again, engaged in the unbelievable. A woman posted the ad just twenty-minutes before I found it online. The pooch made a difference in my life. Like a man and a woman, a woman and a woman or a man and a man, people's life circumstances brought the two together. Immediately, I called for the dog. She gave away a two-year-old canine who was mixed between a chihuahua and a dachshund. I named her Pearl. She was sweet just like Rusty. She had caused problems in the young women's home, however. I saw that Pearl was loved immensely by her. But, she had a boyfriend who was six-four, weighed three-hundred pounds. When she arrived at the location where we met, I looked at her holding the pet. The woman's face looked pained. She looked like she had cried. Her boyfriend, however, looked angry. She asked me if I would give her beloved dog a lot of petting. I told that I would. She handed her to me. It was a wonderful moment for me. My *m-workers*, unbeknownst to me, cheered the arrival. Her *m-workers* consoled her sadness. The reason that she gave her away, I soon learned, was that Pearl was not housetrained, and she wasn't leash trained. She had never been taken on a walk. I put two and two together. The huge boyfriend stepped into her poop, again. It most likely happened before, and she was warned the next time… Well, it was the next time… I successfully housetrained her. She accompanied me as I "traveled" north.

I liked my room at John's. It was on the second floor; his was on the first. I moved all of my possessions, which included my, by this time, medical marijuana, up the stairs. We got along before he went into the hospital. We crossed on the ferry in his car. My rental car remained on the island. We shopped and returned home. He never came onto me, sexually, after the first night. Retrospectively, I was glad. I was less interested in it, for some reason. I picked him up at the hospital and took him home. I never paid him any rent. I drove up, at my expense, but at his request. The whole thing was crazy, but I never realized it as it happened. I took care of his dog and his home while he was in the hospital. I assisted him as a caregiver for two-days. I bathed him, dried him, I even clipped his disgusting toenails. Next thing that I knew, as we ate dinner, he asked me for money. I put down my fork and said: "What?"

Later, it registered in my mind that he screwed me because I learned of his ongoing hobby. He had other people who emailed him about the Island. I heard him, downstairs, on his computer. He drank from a bottle of wine, as he hooted and hollered at pornographic images from the Internet. It exposed to me that I wasn't the first person he did this to because he had my images, too.

I realized, later, it was all a part of my ongoing project by *Mead* and the *m-team* because shit happened, on the island, the next day. He agreed to look at something that I wrote. I brought my laptop into his bedroom. Suddenly, I tripped over something. The laptop flew out of my hands and crashed into one of his large "expensive" vases on the floor. It broke apart and laid in ruin. John never asked me if I was okay when I fell. He just flipped out and started screaming at me.

"Look what you did! Look at what you fucking did! Either you pay me six-hundred dollars or I want you out of my house! I don't want to look at your goddamn laptop or anything you wrote! I want you out!"

I ringed my hands and the little bit of hair that I had. I stormed upstairs in distress. I had to get out of there, but to where. It was so sudden and so distressing. I looked at Pearl and cried. I couldn't afford a room at an establishment. But, I needed out, even if it meant that I was homeless. John knew the VA system. He told me he knew someone who obtained housing through the VA in Tacoma. I worried as we ferried across the ocean. Pearl and I sat in the rental car while we crossed the icy waters. I had loaded some of my possessions into the vehicle even though most of my things remained on the island. John allowed me to put most of it into his garage. Pearl and I drove, unbelievably, around

Tacoma for two-days in the rental car because I couldn't find the homeless shelter. I stopped many times and asked but I never found it. As it turned out I looked for the wrong street. There were two Harvest Streets, one north of downtown, and one south of it. For two nights we slept in the cold car at the parking lot of a *Mcdonald's*.

Later, I credited *Mead* for it all: The tour around Tacoma. The Internet connection. My trip north. The island, John, and all of his antics. It happened too much for me to ignore. In particular, the timing when I tripped, and destroyed his "expensive" vase. I never imagined the unbelievable series of events which followed. When we finally arrived at the shelter the staff member, who processed me, looked at me and said: "You don't have any drugs. I don't have to search your bags." Once again, *m-workers* intervened because I had an ounce of marijuana in one of my bags. Mead blinded me to it while I was at the shelter. There were no cluster headaches. But I wanted to make sure I still had it. I looked through all of my bags and I never found what I looked for. But it was there the whole time, because, weeks later, when I was about to leave, I found it.

Soon, after I arrived at the shelter, I took public transportation to the VA Medical Campus. Cindy Kazel worked at the VA for ten-years. She helped homeless veterans. I was homeless, but I wasn't sure about my status or anything at that point.

But, then it all happened. It was *Mead*. There was no doubt, I said to myself years later. I walked nearer to the solution of my angst over all of these years that day. Cindy asked me a question from a form she filled out: "How would you describe your quality of life?" Immediately, I teared up. It must have pushed my buttons because, uncharacteristically, I shot back: "Are you kidding me?" I talked about my life outside of my work when I was employed in the MH field. I told her that

I had a very empty life. Then she asked me if I had a service connected disability, and if I ever applied for one. I told her about the sexual assaults, and how they impacted my life for fifty-years. She asked: "No family, friends or romance?" "My family doesn't care about me. I am friendly to all people, but I have no friends. As for romance, I told her, "I never had a relationship." "Have you applied for a service connected disability?" "I applied twice and they were both denied." "Well, you need to see a VA compensation specialist," she advised. I said: "It'll just be denied again because there's no proof except the history of my life." I told her about John and how I "traveled" from Las Vegas. She asked: "Is that where you applied for it?" I answered "yes." She replied; "Well, we do things a little differently around here."

I recognized, when I thought about it, years later, that my demeanor in MH, which I used for thirty-years, kicked in while I lived at the shelter. The mood, the confidence, and the kindness drove me just like it did before. Although, I helped only one person in a case manager type situation while I was there… Pearl and I got along with everyone who we encountered.

I arrived at the single story structure. Many men waited in the cold. People's frigid breaths met up with the cigarette smoke that arose in their midst. I looked at the faces of the unfortunate as I sat on a bench next to another. Mike was from Tacoma. His wife threw him out when he returned home drunk one night. He asked me what my dog's name was. "Pearl," I said: "She's beautiful," he said as he petted the mutt. Poverty and despair were evident in the buzz of men's murmured voices; it all looked and sounded so dark. The VA compensation specialist met with me that night. She completed paperwork as she asked me questions.

Once at the homeless shelter it never entered my mind to go back to Las Vegas. I waited in limbo for housing. They gave me a mat and a blanket. Pearl slept at my feet on the floor. To me, as I looked back, the magic was too unbelievable. Remarkable things happened. What amazed me the most was the way everything was timed and fell into place. *Mead*, obviously, wanted me to go through a lot of hoops. I never dreamt that my trip north led to financial security. But it did, and it changed my life. I never questioned anything that happened at that time. Just like in my early years, I was not in control of events. I turned in the mat and blanket when I was told that I could move into the veterans room. There were nine beds and nine vets. The guys loved Pearl. She slept in their beds. Five weeks passed and one night I collapsed at the shelter. An ambulance was called, and I was rushed to a local hospital. Once there, they, soon after, released me. It was one-o'clock in the morning as I walked back to the shelter. I collapsed again, this time on a residential sidewalk. I couldn't get up. I laid there for a period of time. All of the sudden I heard a voice. It was a man and he asked me what was wrong. I told him that I collapsed and I couldn't get up. He picked me up and I was on my feet. The guy, who I never saw, walked away. I only walked ten-paces before I collapsed again. I must have fallen asleep because when I opened my eyes it was daylight and a woman stood over me with a walkie-talkie. An ambulance came and they took me back to the hospital. I just spent the night where I lied on the sidewalk of a city that had a high crime rate. I was protected by *Mead* that night, I realized later.

I was in the hospital for a week. I had pneumonia. After I was discharged I went back to the shelter. The social worker at the hospital arranged for me and Pearl to fly back to Las Vegas. So, we packed up and left. I helped myself tremendously on my trip north, and I helped someone along the way. The man served during VietNam and he received six-hundred dollars per month from Social Security Disability. I knew there was a program for veterans like him. It guaranteed, a former service member, one-thousand dollars per month. I hooked him up with the VA Compensation Specialist who helped me, and she got on it right away. It was an amount that changed a life. He was due about thirty-thousand dollars, when backdated.

Chapter 24

After Manuel broke Lily's arm and he was banished until he cleaned up his act, she had surveillance cameras installed. They were mounted in five-areas inside and outside of the home. Police found the areas where they were installed. They were ripped from their mountings. The whereabouts of the devices remained unknown. Lily's cell phone was also missing. Detective Jackson and his team scoured the home for a week. They found, absolutely, nothing in the way of physical evidence. Circumstantially there was evidence. Detective Jackson knew of Manuel's assault on Lily, and he obtained information from family members. I told him about Lily's and Manuel's history. He had compiled enough circumstantial evidence that Manuel was called in for his second interrogation. Detective Jackson wanted to break him.

The room had become all too familiar to Manuel. The youth took a seat and glanced up at the surveillance camera. He smiled for a split second. Jackson was joined by another detective, Lenny, who remained silent the entire time that Detective Jackson and Manuel dueled. It was "an Academy Award performance," the silent detective wrote in his notes, which I obtained long after the events. The detective asked: "Manuel tell me what happened from the beginning." The silent detective told me that they typically did that. They looked for inconsistencies. Manuel retold the story; he delivered his words with the expression, which indicated that he'd said the words before. "Like, I already told you, you're wasting my time," Lenny scribbled. There was one area of contention. Where were the surveillance devices and Lily's cell phone. After he finished his recital, Manuel scooted forward and leaned back in the chair. Jackson took the opportunity to cross examine him about the day's interrogation. He compared it to the first. This time he used Manuel's statement that he lived on the other side of the house and that he heard nothing around the time of death the coroner had determined. Manuel's physical communication showed that he was outraged. He scooted back in his seat and sat up. His facial expression indicated his astonishment as the silent detective recounted it.

"So, what are you trying to say, exactly? Manuel asked. "That I had something to do with the murder of my mother. That is an insult. How dare you accuse me. I loved my mother." Jackson brought up Lily's broken arm. Manuel explained the pushing and shoving, and claimed that "it doesn't mean that I murdered the person that I loved. I'd been with her since the age of four. I worshiped my mother. I am offended, frankly. I did not murder her. I loved her with all my heart."

The detectives looked at each other for a second: Detective Jackson looked back at Manuel and told him: "You're good. You are really good."

Manuel exploded; contrition was the last thing on his mind. "I'm good. I'm really good," "Oh, my God, I can't believe this. You think I'm acting?"

Jackson stated simply: 'No, I think you're a sociopath."

"A sociopath? You think that I am a sociopath! I swear. I'm so insulted right now. Don't you understand that I loved her with all of my heart and soul."

Jackson looked at Lenny, who shrugged his shoulders. "Well," Jackson said, "let me tell you what I think really happened that night. You planned it all. You went into the garage and picked up the ax. You sharpened it on a stone just before you used it. You played what you wanted to do over and over in your mind. To you it solved your problem. You talked your way out of things before. You believe that you're good at that. She had crossed the line so many times, you rationalized. You must've moved down the hallway, just like Jack Nickolson in *The Shining*. You were determined to do what needed to be done with your sharpened tool. Your mother was asleep. Her light and television were on. With one swift blow you drove the ax into her skull. Her body convulsed," he said, "then she gurgled. You took all of the CCT equipment, her purse and phone to the lake behind the house. You threw it in. Your phone, boy genius, was in your back pocket. You retrieved it and called 911."

Manuel shook his head, vehemently. "I did not murder my mother."

"Life with your mother was very cordial after you broke her arm. You stopped talking back. You were quieter, I learned from looking at her email to one of her friends. But with each constructive prompt, she gave you, you complied, but at the same time it ratcheted, what you cared for, up a notch. It must've brewed in you for a while. You had a plan. Like I said. You wanted to do what you did, but you did not want to face any consequences for it. In fact, during your first interrogation you wondered if this interfered with your future college plans. So, don't give me that shit that you didn't. Yes, you did. You were in her room. When you were banished from home, she installed an array of security equipment around the house. Cameras, motion detectors, the whole-nine-yards. You knew the equipment was there, Manuel. In fact, after you did it you dismantled all of it. You threw that and her purse into a lake behind the house. Days before you sneaked around. You spied on her that night that she was on the phone with her brother.

Manuel leaned forward and he pointed his finger at Detective Jacson, in a quivered voice he said, emphatically, "I did not murder my mother."

Jackson looked at his partner who shrugged his shoulders. "Okay," the detective came back, "I can see this is going nowhere." Jackson later told his peer: "Since there's no physical evidence, I can't draw a confession out of him. We have no other choice, but to drain the lake." Manuel was released again.

Chapter 25

Pat's alcoholism and her Pliartrum drug addiction took a turn for the worse; she was arrested on a DUI. When she worked she drank and smoked. So, when she got into her car and drove home every night; it happened. Frank bailed her out. When I went to Boris' sentencing hearing, she looked ill. Frank looked embarrassed to be there.

Boris appeared in an orange jump-suit and chains as he entered the courtroom. The teen looked less defiant. He was born Boris Karloff Isaac. Frank told me it was "so cool to pick out a newborn's name." He felt that he honored Boris by giving him the name. "It did," according to Pat. They watched old horror movies from the 1930s and 40s together when he was young. "Frankenstein, The Bride of Frankenstein, and the Son of Frankenstein were honored movies in the household. Boris was a difficult child to raise." He was born unwanted which impacted the family nucleus. He was ignored more than he was loved. He was disciplined and punished almost daily. He was rarely rewarded with something. Frank and Pat raised him like they were raised. They expected him to succeed, but he skirted their expectations. He dropped out of high school in the tenth-grade. "But he earned his GED," she defended. The boy stood taller than Frank, who was six-feet-three inches. He was good looking and the girls liked him. So, something went wrong in Doctor Frankenstein's laboratory, I thought. When I "traveled" I always made a stop at Frank's. They put me in the extra bedroom once. I stayed in the notorious basement every other time. In the cellar, my cluster headaches and the depression that I felt were very bad. One night, I had a strong cluster headache. I had nothing to fight it with. In addition, my lower back went out, and I had to pee. It was all at the same time. I dragged myself to the bathroom. Without doubt, it could have won the prize as the worst experience in my whole, excuse the profanity, fucking life. One day, in the morning, when I was in the guest room, I heard through my closed bedroom door the struggle between an addicted mother and her dysfunctional son. Pat said things like: "If you don't go to school then you can't have any dessert tonight. I made an apple pie." He retorted: "I don't care. I don't want to go to school." Frank and Pat were pushed to the limit, and attended a number of emergency parent/teacher conferences over the years. The father always told the boy: "I never, in my life, had a parent/teacher conference; emergency or not."

Boris was, according to prison officials, in the early phases of psychosis. It was most uncommon for him to have his first episode before the age of eighteen. It happened, however. When they lived out in Patriot Park, Pat told me that Boris liked to trap small rodents with a cardboard box. One year, Frank bought him a small trap for his birthday. The main problems that Boris had centered around Frank, and his inept parenting. He and Pat's alcoholism, along with her use of Pliartrum's drugs created the perfect storm. They were too loose with Boris. He was allowed to run roughshod in the home. Frank told him: "when you were a youngster a disturbed stork brought you to us." The misshapen mind believed it. When he got older the "philosopher," said one day: "I don't like being human. I'd rather have been a part of the bird or lizard world; he said that it would be "real cool" to be a vulture or a Komodo Dragon.

Boris faced the music that day. It lasted more than an hour. It took place in the same courtroom where he was tried and found guilty. Boris faced the death penalty or life in prison without parole. I talked to him about it. Because his mother and father never did, since the guilty verdict. They never loved him, and they showed it. Sarah was off at college. She was in her freshman's year, studying to be a nurse, something she always wanted to be.

My presence, at the sentencing hearings, helped nothing. The youngman's eyes looked defeated. The Honorable Judge who rose above him entered, which followed the Bailiff's announcement. We all stood until the judge took his seat and gaveled in. The court sentencing allowed different family and friends, who were unbelievably broken-hearted, over the manner of their loved one's deaths. For people who died because of natural causes, or even after a long illness; it was easier to cope with. When murdered, everyone, who knew the victim, felt horrible, as if it had happened to them.

Boris sat, nervously, at his Defense Council's table. His head darted like a dog. He was flanked by his attorney, a public defender. The prosecutor sat adjacent to the defense. He represented the State. I sat in the courtroom crowded by the press, family and friends of the deceased.

I thought about it. It sent my mind back to the time I watched the full interrogation of Boris. Detective Wicks was the best interrogator. He was fantastic. He circled the boy like he was a giant anaconda and it wrapped around its prey before he went in for the kill. He stroked the boy's ego from the second he walked into that interrogation room. He soon got him to talk. The detective told Boris: "Wow! You're confident, cool, and very unique. Where did you obtain the knowledge to do all of this? Were you watching stuff?" "No," Boris replied, "the knowledge just comes to me." He went on: "I've developed myself as an assassin."

"Did you have training?" he asked the boy.

"No; it was sheer mental imagination," he replied.

"Where did you get the knife?" Wicks inquired.

"From my Aunt Glenda," he said

The Judge looked like a learned man. His white hair and low brow fit the ambiance. He sat down and read paperwork. He picked up a pair of glasses, put them on. His entire being moved closer, to the information, as he focused on what he read. The murmured voices were silenced after he hit and gaveled in with three punishing blows to the bench. Family and friends of the victim stood and took the stand. One member presented their soul to the Court in place of the beloved woman who was of very old age. "Take me," she cried. Boris shook his head, I remembered.

The Prosecution's recommendations were firm: death. "Is the public defender prepared to argue? The lawyer stood and, basically, argued that Boris presented a danger to society but that his life should be spared because he's a juvenile. "This is the result of a neglected child. He was raised poorly. His father never loved him. His mother; well, that's a different story. Pat told me that when she became pregnant; she wanted the child; it was the father who didn't. After she became pregnant, they married. There was always a conflict between the father and the son; it only became worse as he aged. When he was born he was a burden in his father's eyes. So, when it came to parenting, the Public Defender explained, financially, they spent little on the boy; he went without. Clothes, dentist, doctors; it all added up. Frank neglected his son. In those formidable years, Frank was more interested in Pliartrum than he was in son. The father took his frustrations out of the boy. The mother's love was too weak to overcome the powerful punishment of the child by the father, who was just doing the right thing, when he took on the role of Dad. But he never, really, wanted the part. He never, actually, shirked away from his responsibility of producing the child. The young killers' mind was a piece of clay and it was a misshapen mess. The parents never lifted a finger. Finances weren't spent on him. They only took him to the dentist once. The boy never received instructions. He was left to figure out life on his own. His goodness and other important aspects of his life went undeveloped, as a result. You want to, really, know what went wrong with my client, just turn on the television, or go to a movie or just hop on the Internet. Disturbing messages and images are being sent to their fertile minds. "The defendant will rise," the judge said. Boris stood..

The Judge cleared his voice and announced: "The jury has found you guilty in the murder of Betty Laslo, in the first degree with malice. I understand the defendant has something to say before I rule."

The Defender looked at Boris for a second. "Your Honor, I realize that I'm here for you to impose my punishment. All I can say is that it's hard." Boris turned around with contempt written all over his face; he said: "You're all fools."

The Judge gaveled in, several times, as the uniformed court personnel, two junior staffers, took action. Boris was physically prompted to sit. Once seated, the court's workhorses remained in place with their hands on the shoulders of the defendant. The Judge read from his prepared remarks. "The defendant has not convinced this court that you understood the gravity of your actions." He looked up and said: "Your latest outburst only strengthens that finding. You're a very ill, young man. But, you knew right from wrong, and, yet, you pursued the wrong. I find no extenuating circumstances. "Boris Karloff Isaac, having been found guilty of this heinous crime I sentence you to be put to death."

Boris lifted his arm far enough, and he gave the Judge the finger. The wise man ignored him. He rose and left the courtroom. I watched Boris as the two courthouse law enforcers lifted him out of his seat; each had a hold of an arm and they led him away. He dragged his legs so they were forced to lift him. He smiled on his way out. He looked just like *Norman Bates* at the end of *"Psycho."*

Chapter 26

Detective Jackson had a theory. He believed that a person who broke the law, murdered another and was conscious free, lived a life void of guilt because they feared nothing. Their minds were cleared. They never looked over their shoulders to see if they're being followed. The guilty, like this one, never believed that he could be in any trouble. His whole being rejected any sense of emotion or even awareness about it. There was no pride. There were no celebrations. It happened just as if he got in and out of his clothes everyday. He never thought about it. He just did it. If they went away to school or the military they had no fear that they faced any trouble from their past. They're very good at burying it. It was as if the crime never occurred. Nothing happened in their minds after it. It's over, move on. *Mead* provided another path. If only the person knew that they were being tested. Maybe, they'd think differently. If he took the path, he was toast.

"Manuel was a one man wrecking crew," Jackson said. While he and his partner, Lenny, surveyed the lake, they stood behind Lily's home. The small lake was being drained. It took six-months, but they nabbed their man. Lenny submitted a request for Manuel's cell-phone carrier to provide the records; it took forever to compile it. Detective Jackson had Manuel under surveillance twenty-four seven.

He was not permitted back at his home; it was still considered a crime scene. The teen stayed at a friend's house. What went on according to reports. He went on with his life, according to Lenny. He went to stores. He went to movies and restaurants. He played basketball hoops outside with his friend. He even took out the trash once.

The third interrogation followed up three-weeks later. This time, Manuel was arrested. Jackson led his team to bring him in. He sat in the same seat; in the same interrogation room. He was very relaxed before. He was free of any criminal jewelry. But, today, he wore handcuffs behind his back. Manuel's mood and demeanor were quite different the third time around. Jackson sank his teeth into him. The evidence became the club which the detective used to bludgeon him. Manuel looked more defiant than he was defeated at first. The amount of evidence that they lacked, and they hoped to find was, finally, compiled into one big giant punch in Manuel's gut. He listened for an hour as Jackson screamed at him about all of the evidence. The detective's manner was so harsh, Manuel began to cry with his chin on his chest. Whether the sociopath felt anything but pity for himself was unknown. He, eventually, lifted his head and started to talk. He confessed, but his story changed over the weeks and months; he was less culpable because of his mental health and abuse. I never knew for sure that a person with mental illness, for the most part, knew the difference between right and wrong except when their mind is in the throes of psychosis. If the individual was sick with that, they were insane. But, evil was certainly not insane. And this was just plain evil.

A trial followed because of Manuel's plea, in spite of his confession. He changed his plea from guilty to not guilty by reason of insanity. The jury took only a few hours until they reached a verdict. Manuel stood with his head down. He heard the words. I knew that he was on antipsychotic medication; which was new. He was only diagnosed and treated for depression before. The killer had gone misdiagnosed since childhood. Manuel received the kind of important resources from Lily that Frank never provided for Boris. Yet they both landed themselves in the worst position a human has to tolerate. He was sent to prison. He received no allowance for being underage. In fact, it led, very early on, for Manuel to fight for his manhood. He stemmed from pure machismo. He protected himself from sexual assault so many times that it got to the point that he, for a month, stayed in solitary confinement.

I never visited Manuel. We never exchanged email. I was the absent uncle. Just like Uncle Stu was to me. Lily had her hands full; I should've connected more with them, and that sort of thing was what bothered me most, my inability to connect with family or any normal people. I didn't beat mental illness, I fought it. It won most of the time. I have resigned myself to what occurred. My sister, Lily, was the only soul, besides Mom-Mom, that I ever felt anything for. She was very carefree, and to imagine what happened to her always unsettled me.

Chapter 27

I flew back to Las Vegas. Pearl needed a small pet-carrier. *Mead* understood that I was incapable of doing anything for myself, which I believed at the time. *M-workers* enlisted two men who assisted without me asking. They, really, did all the work as I watched. Pearl was such a gentle dog, but she was also stubborn. I never feared that she was vicious. I departed the plane with Pearl in one bag. I had the marijuana too; it was checked in. I checked out without a problem.

Soon after all of this I got a letter from the VA. I was to meet with a private-psychologist who contracted with them. She interviewed me, regarding my service-connected disability. When I left her office that day I expected a long wait until a decision came down. She estimated that it might be a six-month wait. They had to do a deep dive until they determined my fate.

Six-months passed, then seven, eight and nine; nothing. One day, in the tenth-month, I received two envelopes: I presumed that one announced their decision. The other; it was from the U.S. Treasury. The amount of money changed my life. It also kindled me. It started a small flame that reignited a symptom of my bipolar. I spent a lot. I lost, virtually, every possession to that guy on the island. While I was in the hospital I got a call from him. He told me that if I didn't come for my possessions within the week my stuff would be thrown out. I told him that I would come for them, but I never did. I abandoned it all. Frankly, I didn't care so much when I received my VA disability because everything he had was what I "traveled" with. The possessions went from State to State. They filled the backseat of the car, practically, to the top. There was only an inch or two above it. I required the rearview mirror. Some of the clothes dated back decades that I carted around for tens-of-thousands of miles. Most of them were skinny clothes. And I was skinny at that time. But, it never lasted. In fact, I've spent, over the last fifty-years, more time being obese than thin. So, the clothes meant nothing to me. I was, actually, glad because I was rid of them. Back in Las Vegas with Pearl I looked for places to move to. I wanted to move out of the State, and relocate somewhere along the coast of the Pacific Northwest.

I don't know when Gilbert placed the ad. My future landlord renovated an old motel from the 1930s. It was on the market for decades. There were nine-suits. One room had the kitchen and living room. The other was the bedroom and the bathroom. The rooms were perfect for me and Pearl, it was also very affordable. Gilbert didn't want a pet deposit, which most other rentals did, especially in an apartment community. The town sat along the rugged Pacific coast. There were about five-thousand people, ten-thousand dogs and thirty-six-thousand birds.

Everything changed for me and Pearl. But, before we arrived at my newest location, I drove over one-thousand miles from Nevada up to Washington, two very strange occurrences happened. The first night we stayed somewhere. I drove nearly thirty-thousand miles and I never, ever slept in the car. I was flush with money from the VA, yet, we did. We slept in the car. I never explained it to myself; it was unnecessary and crazy. Five-o'clock in the morning we got back on the highway. I drove for two-hours; I was dazed. I saw a sign. It directed me to my location. It was up the side of a mountain. Picture rocks-sized softballs on an unpaved road that snaked around the side of it. Immediately, I spoke to Pearl. "Oh, my God," that's how scared I was but I kept going, and I continued: "Oh, my God." There was snow on the mountain. There were no other cars or people. When I looked to my left I must have been up three-thousand feet. I drove a truck, something I purchased with my disability money. I had never owned a pick-up truck, yet I bought one. As it started to snow, I attempted to back the vehicle up. I attempted the maneuver. I never turned it around. I got the back tire stuck in a ditch in the mud. There was no way out. We were three-thousand feet up the side of a mountain, and it snowed, I had no cell phone service.

I was stuck.

I got out of the car once. I thought I'd walk down the mountain's rocky road to get help. I never made it. It snowed hard. I walked about five minutes and determined that it was not safe. I couldn't make it. *M-workers* issued a warning, which transmitted to me that if I went any further I was in trouble because, my voice said to me, if you fall, you will not get up. I struggled to get back, as twilight approached, and I did. We spent the night there. I turned on the engine every twenty-minutes to warm up the cab. I was soaked by the snow. The car's heater dried my clothes. The next morning, I thought that I needed to try. The only way to get help was to go down the mountain. It was around ten-o'clock, and the sky was clear. Suddenly, I heard an engine. I kicked open the passenger side door. It was another vehicle. The man worked for the County and he came up to measure the snowpack. He told me that he'd found people dead before in the cars. He looked at my situation, and the guy pulled me out; he even turned the truck around for me.

Pearl and I went down the side of the mountain quickly thereafter. I never knew the man's name but I thanked him very much. But, what the County Worker did, I thought, was the beginning of my awareness that something consistently happened to me. *It* saved me from danger and trouble too many times. When I collapsed in Tacoma at one-o'clock in the morning, I laid there all night. Something protected me. I began to investigate things that I never investigated before. I never knew why I was so isolated. The issue still bothered me. I did okay, most of the time, when I was alone. Sometimes, however, I pouted and complained.

Why was I so immoral in my youth? It wasn't that I felt guilt. I worked for nearly thirty-years, on and off, in a field that treated and restored minds. My mind was in need of knowledge. Then, eventually, I figured it out. Before that, however, I thought about it a lot. But I never found any answers. Years passed before I came across what I thought were two diagnoses that, flatley, I didn't need to look at, I used to tell myself. It was impossible that I, diagnostically, had them. I believed that I never met the criteria for Schizoid Personality Disorder, SPD or Antisocial Personality Disorder, ASPD. They were just diagnostic titles to me. I had no reason, ever, to read further. I thought SPD, related to people with schizophrenia. When it came to ASPD, I thought it applied to someone who was psychotic or a sociopath. When I bothered, for the first time in my life, to read just what exactly happened if someone had SPD or ASPD. When I searched, which was not until long after the bipolar diagnosis, I never learned the specifics. I studied it, after I settled into my new surroundings. I self-diagnosed but there were no questions. I had both SPD and ASPD. Along with bipolar, I had one hell of a trifecta, I thought. Both diagnoses fit me like a glove. They explained why I did what I did as a teenager. It explained why I was so isolated. That I sought no friends; I never had romance; I was always estranged from my family. My puzzle was complete. I researched and watched Youtube videos, which helped me. I now understood.

A lot of things went wrong in my development. I recognized how dysfunctional I really was. I explained to myself that this was SPD, and that was ASPD. I had a lot of this and that. The one thing that got me was *Mead*. After the knowledge was presented to me, I thought a lot about it. I did my homework, and it helped me immensely. I rebounded like never before. I now felt comforted by isolation. Being alone was okay. I confronted my sexuality. I was instructed about it, but I never followed it. Now, it was okay that I was friendless, even though I was always friendly to people. It was, finally, okay for me to say: "I stay to myself." As far as the ASPD, it doesn't haunt me, but that's part of the problem given the diagnosis. Both Mom and Dad were dead and buried before I learned of my situation in life. It's made a world of difference. Once I understood I was released. I was freed. I was happy. I liked myself. I treated myself with dignity and respect; something I refused to do all of my life. Once I had a client, at one of my MH jobs, who asked me about something she experienced. When she described it I understood. At one point when I "traveled" I became so ill that the same thing happened to me. The sensation took place in the palm of one's hand. When in the throes of very deep depression something happened. I felt something; it came from the inside out. Something that poked a few times; it felt like the head of a ballpoint pen. It was as if it knocked on a palm like a door; it wanted out. Years later, I understood; it was the soul that knocked and it sent a message; it rejected self, our physical being, our vehicle for life.

Chapter 28

Once a year, I visited Boris in Altoona, Pennsylvania, at the State Prison. He lost two appeals, but he rallied support for clemency. The twenty-six year old had many close shaves, but nothing panned out. His case was in the hands of the Supreme Court. The last time I saw him. He stepped into the "metal box," as he called it. We were separated by thick glass. We each picked up the phone receiver. I thought it was time that we had a heart-to-heart talk. He never knew that I was mentally ill, and that I worked, most of my life, in that field of work. I wrote to him and I told that I was bipolar, which was diagnosed by the VA, but that I self diagnosed that I had SPD and ASPD. I wanted him to know about my criminality. Since he never knew about me, and because he spent more quality time with his Aunt Glenda as a kid, he heard the truth from me, just like the kids in school, I told him things that began to sink in.

He never understood ASPD. "It's triggered through a person's genetics and environment," I told him. "But," I added; "it never meant what you did was forgivable. You're still responsible. You were given the path to do it because you yearned for it. You played with it in your mind. You incorporated it.into your personality. You should've used your right and wrong skills and not gotten on it in the first place. But, you did. You hopped aboard. You could have stopped at any time while you were on your way. Before you acted, but you didn't, so you failed. You were being tested. I know it was a powerful urge. You should have ignored it because you knew that it was wrong." Boris broke eye contact with me and he looked down. I thought, at that moment, that he understood. He was heavily medicated with psychotropic medications. After a minute he looked me in the eyes and said: "Thank you."

Boris had his supporters. He found religion over the last decade. He made contact with two Rabbis who sent letters of support to the Governor. They asked for a reprieve based on the man's age when the crime occurred. They pleaded to reduce his sentence to life without parole. They claimed that his remorse was genuine and that he recognized he was seriously mentally ill, but that he took responsibility for his actions. The Rabbis also sought support from one of the State's House of Representatives. Unfortunately, he was a member of the Country Club Party, and he refused to even see them. The People Party House Member invited him to his local office and his assistant listened, but her support could not stop his final appeal. He had received a reprieve twice over the decade he sat on the death row. Through those years Boris had his ups and downs. The Rabbis provided the prayers for the dead. They acted to comfort the young man. I, however, never thought, what happened next.

Boris told me that he had a girlfriend. He said that she wrote him a letter after he was sentenced, and, according to him, they hit it off. They write letters to each other each week. She lived in Ohio. She worked as a lab technician at one of Pliatrum's pain centers. They shared an interest in politics. Pliartrum kindled love, he brought the two lovebirds together.

Frank told me the young killer wrote to him. He said that he found religion and espoused Pliartrumism. He never pitied the boy, "they were just words," he said. Then he insulted me because, he said, of my constant rants and how dangerous Pliartrum was. Again, I feared not, and I amplified my support for Lily, and the People Party, and my hatred for Pliartrum and the Country Club Party. "If God only knew."

Later, I realized that *Mead* was up to its normal antics. *It* created conflict in the world, so often, over mankind's existence it's countless. But, I understood why. Exactly, what happened to America during Pliartrum's term in Office was all courtesy of *Mead*, because the Country, just like Germany, of the 1930s, followed the Pied Piper into the river of raw sewage.

It was years ago. But, "however many years later," I told him, "this country is resilient; it always has been," I said, "the American people should've never allowed organized crime to get their foot into the door of the Federal Government in the first place; but the mob and it allies hoodwinked the people "Pliartrum was kin to the most evil force in the Universe." That the words the former president used were rooted in Satanism. But the country wasn't left unsheltered. It held up long enough for him and his Country Clubs Party's goons to try again. I emphasized, however, in the long run, democracy and truth won. They tried awfully hard, and I could be wrong when it's all said and done. They almost succeeded at times, but the People Party prevailed because of our innate abilities to stand for democracy. We always persevered. We, Frank, the country, the people, we're simply a hostage to the former so-called Commander in Chief.

"Under Pliartrum, the US suffered," I pronounced to Frank's defiant eyes, "his four-years in the White House, and his "post-presidency," told it all. I said, "it didn't matter what happened next. The damage had been done. America would never be the same because of Pliartrum, his family, friends, those, political and non-political hacks, and all of his merry goons who supported, aided and abetted his criminality. It was just like the time that he built that retreat/casino. The mob had it built, they milked it dry, and it went into bankruptcy. When he took the Oval Office, there was a photo taken by the Russian media, the US media were denied access, but, even so, the photo generated much more than a thousand words. It was more like a million.

Pliartrum robbed the Treasury; and crippled the IRS. He attempted to destroy the Justice Department, and hobbled homeland security. He wanted to dismantle NATO. The idiot president placed the country's intelligence and law enforcement entities, namely, the FBI, CIA, NTF, as well as the Secret Service, into grave danger. The organized crooks took control of the Federal Government; it was like magic to Pliartrum. The Federal government, however, was in grave danger if, God forbid, Pliartrumism continued. He was in bed with all of the crooks of the World, he always was. They and Pliartrum aimed for glory. They expected, insisted and instituted organized-crime like methods and practice, with the goal of World domination.

Lily wrote in her comment on Youtube: *Don't let organized crime rule America*. I thought about it and decided that she should've added: *Don't let organized crime rule the World.* "They want to make the United States an oligarchical system, just like Russia. Washington, D.C. would be called "little Moscow." People like Lily and I stood up for Democracy and the Constitution. We were against authoritarianism and mob-rule economy. Our feet were planted. We held the signs at demonstrations that were on the side of peace and tolerance, and against Pliartium, hate and organized crime. As I drove to the airport for a flight, I thought about my nephew. I told myself that I should've been a better uncle.

Chapter 29

Lily told Frank that he abandoned the truth when he supported Pliartrum. "He's killing this country," she said, long before J6. It began innocently. My brother's admiration for the loudmouth thug. "He watched his television show every week," Pat told me. He once explained, to me, before the hostility and J6, that Pliartrum recharged him. He told me that he felt powerful feelings that he never had before. He turned on his favorite newscast, each night, which was anchored by his favorite family member. PROX News had a grip on Frank's testicles even before Pliartrum entered the Oval Office. He watched Glenda and absorbed every talking point. With his heightened cynicism he shouted words of encouragement at her on the television, especially when she had a segment on the president's son, according to Pat. Demonization became a hobby for Frank. He thought people should help themselves. I asked him: "What's wrong with the government helping people in need?" He shot back like a Pliartrum stooge: "What do you want me to do about it?"

In 2016 I lived in another State but I kept contact with Frank, all thru Pliartrum's first term in office. To Frank and his core cohorts, the fantastic five, which was what I called them, it all started out like one-big-joke. Frank loved the way Pliartrum pushed back at the press. Frank hated the legitimate press. He disliked it because Pliartrum did. He was one-hundred percent Glenda and PROX News, who he deemed "the only source for truth." A spell was casted over him. Overnight, it seemed, he transformed himself. He was no longer the tall skinny kid without a care in the world. He never was political before Pliartrum, but he signed up right away to be a Pliartrum canvasser for the president. He attended meetings and socialized a great deal. The main course in this dastardly meal was hatred towards every Federal Institution which enforced laws. Hatred for Blacks and illegal immigrants, gays, lesbians and transgender. I never heard a discouraging word out of Frank about hating Jews. But, I told him, his association with Pliartrum and his people, said a lot about him in that department. In the early part of Pliartrum's term we'd talk for an hour.

He presented his talking points, and I presented mine. We were civil. We let each other talk. We said nice things to each other in between all of the Pliartrum talk. But, as the years passed, we talked less. And when we did talk there were fireworks. His tone was loud; it never was before. He was smitten with Pliartrum. Later, he took on a dedication to the former president that impacted his wife and children. Pat went to the bottle more. Sarah went to her friend's house. It was all to drown out Frank's radicalism.

On weekends it was nothing but Pliartrum. From 2017 when Pliartrum took Office, to 2018, Frank was with his "group," Keith, Don, Catch and Sammy. The fivesome fed off each other with their beer bottles in hand at the bar in the basement. Each week they gathered to talk about Pliartrum and about all of the people who he, and they hated. They, without doubt, were all good heterosexual family men. In fact, when I "traveled" that year back east I stayed at Frank's. One day, in the basement, Keith was there with his young son. When I came down the stairway, a funny thing happened. I told Frank in the 1990s that I was gay. He paused on the phone when I said it. And then he told everyone. A secret that I kept because of my shame was now a piece of candy to all of the haters. When I said hello to Keith, he said nothing, and pulled his young son closer to him. I ignored it, and I got what I needed from the downstairs refrigerator. I went back upstairs.

Pat told me that Frank paid more attention to Pliartrum than he did to his family. They took trips to the ocean in the summer every year when Boris was incarcerated on death-row. Now, they went to Pliartrum rallies. "You'll have a lot of fun," he told Sarah. Pat pulled Sarah closer to her. They went to three-rallies. "Two were on a tar-mack in the summer, and one, the most memorable, took place in forty-degree weather in the middle of a cornfield in 2020 in upstate New York," Frank, paid their twenty-dollar Pliartrum parking fee, which the candidate proclaimed was a donation to his campaign in 2020. Frank had already given Pliartrum money, and he was encouraged by his supervisors from the governor's office, to set up an automatic deduction once per month. That's when Lily looked closer. Pliartrum was a crook. All of his pain centers and pain retreats were tax-havens for the so-called billionaire. Pliartrum took a cut of everything. When a company approached him for the rights to sell Pliartrum trading cards. He received a cool million, Lily thought, which, she said, "he also received a cool million from several people that he pardoned before he left office, and another million for him and Rich, Jr.. They offered color-commentary to a judo event in Hong Kong.

Hundreds of Pliartrum's people were brewing. They went through security, and, quickly, the area cordoned off with yellow tape filled up like a rock concert. Whenever I talked to Frank, I knew that I talked with Glenda and Uncle Stu at the same time. She added that they had to park a mile away from the rally site. The wind was terrific, she said. Pliartrum arrived by helicopter, spoke his usual rant for forty-minutes, he got back in the helicopter and took off. There were no buses or shuttles to and from the rally site. "We were freezing as we walked the mile back to the pick-up truck, which was parked in a cornfield," she recollected. Sarah never endured the trip because she went to her friend's house that weekend; her "safe house."

Before the 2020 Presidential Election, in 2018, Pliartrum lost his Country Club majorities in both the House of Representative and the Senate. Frank devoted all of his free time to Pliartrum's campaign. Besides canvassing, he also became a troll. Pliartrum's people gave him names and email addresses, and he sent messages in the name of Pliartrum, to households all over the State. In them, he harassed voters for their devotion to the People Party, as well as their feelings toward the former leader. Frank never told me if he had ever made threats in his communiques. I would have said, no way, before Pliartrum. Now, I wouldn't put it past him."

I thought, once, if I could clap my hands or ring a bell, I would do so, to break the spell that Frank, Uncle Stu, and a lot of good Americans who were under the power of Glenda, with her PROX news mishegoss and Pliartrum. As the 2020 election drew closer I used every argument I thought of. I asked my brother: "Can you imagine your grandchildren's future, under Pliartrum, and his ilk, where it's organized crime who rules America." He would simply use another one of Glenda/Pliartrum's talking points. The dishonesty and thuggery of Pliartrum, and, in turn, the Country-Club Party members was so blatant, that I knew it was Mead. The old country-club members, who still cared about this country, and who wanted to continue with our form of government. Pliartrum people were blinded by *m-workers*, who acted on orders. *Mead* wanted to test each person's morality levels, just like it was done to the German people back in the 1930s.

Pliartrum's message spread throughout the land like a virus. To me it was as bad as the pandemic. A lot of innocent people could lose their lives, once again, thanks to Glenda, PROX News, and the former dimwit.

The night of the 2020 Presidential Election, Glenda interviewed Pliartrum. He never touted that he simply would go away, lick his wounds, and live to fight another day. "But that's not Pliartrum," Lily told me. "He announced the night the election was stolen from him, even before the results were announced. He had done it before. When he ran in

2016, he did the exact same thing. He announced on a talk show, a few months before the election, that if he didn't win then it was stolen from him. That's because, Lily told me, "he's the leader of organized crime in America. He's never going to abandon that. He was only a toy-soldier before he received the Country Club nomination in 2016. "When he won," Lily said, "He had real power for four-years, but he knew nothing about government or the Presidency. He only knew how to use "muscle." He was a dunce and a thug, and, thanks to *Mead*, he got past the law, who should've been on his ass for all of his crimes decades ago. But, *Mead* had other motives, I believed. For example: The feds were blinded; Pliartrum skirted the IRS by dumping hundreds of thousands of documents attached to income tax returns each year, too many for anyone to go through, so they always accepted his word."

In his first term, he was a piece of driftwood in an ocean. He never learned how to drive the damn thing. The country gets by because of his ineptness. The guy was all brawn. He copied his heroes, the mafia thugs of yesteryear, who all ended up in prison, which was where Lily thought he should've been long ago, along with every last elected official who was in cahoots with him on *J6*. There were many, and each Country Club House Member and those in the Senate who held office, must face legal consequences for fraud against the American People, Lily felt. Not one should be allowed to serve in the United States government again. The other thug organizations: Pee-Boys, Nazis and a host of other scum, who lived under a rock, and, for the first time, they had a soapbox thanks to technology, and it was their man in power. Pliartrum's crookedness rivaled that of Tutin in Russia, who he bowed to and kissed his ring. Later, as all crooks eventually do, he messed up. He miscalculated and it opened the door for Pliartrum, not only to be, possibly, the President of the United States, and the leader of organized crime in America, he now saw himself, with Tutin in trouble, as the Leader of organized crime in the world. President Rich Pliartrum saw himself as the most powerful man in human history.

Pliartrum triggered a mass psychosis in America, that happened in the Country's history. The civil war was not triggered by a psychopath. This megalomaniac was an idiot that the World, yet alone the States, had not seen since the likes of Adolf Hitler. And the good common sense people of America understood. But Lily believed that Pliartrum was the kind of person, when he tasted real power, it was, in his mind, forever. He looked upon himself as a historic figure who stood out. In his mind he was right up there with Gengas Khan, Alexander the Great and Napoleon. "He became, in his mind," Lily said: "*The Godfather* of organized crime in the country." Lily's Youtube video comment and his post that followed it, proved it. He had a serious mental illness on top of it all. Lily once told me that if he won the Oval Office, again, it would take a swat-team to get him out of there.

When Frank was a boy scout. Mom thought he needed a father figure. She knew the scout leader, so she enrolled him. Frank earned many merit badges. What he picked up helped him and he grew. He discovered that he loved politics. One night he was introduced to the Country Club party, he was smitten with it. As a county tax-collector, he formed opinions about his fellow man. He used to be timid when we were young. His timidity shifted to cynicism and hostility towards others. Pliartrum's hate and cruelty was a drug to him and he felt empowered by it.

The years went by. Pliartrum's election bid failed. It wasn't the first time in World History that I thought about. They perverted mankind. Their philosophy was extended to the masses. *Mead* in consultation with the *Executives*, who sought guidance from *God*, which, with misfortune, a decision to see, ultimately, if *Mead* was ordered to have the *m-team* construct a path to teach the ultimate lesson to mankind once again. *M-watchers* ordered *m-workers* to create a path for the madness of a people to carry out the unthinkable. Another path was for the poor souls that passed through the horror. It happened. The groups were there. The atmosphere caused the minds of the people to be triggered. It took one man, Adolf Hitler, to pull it. *Mead*, through Hitler, tested modern mankind; it failed miserably.

Sarah spent a lot of time at the Sherman residence. Her friend, Cindy, was a wonderful pianist. She lived in a large brick home, not far from where we grew up. It was in a nice section of the town. Her dad was a doctor, and her mom a volunteer worker at a nursing home. The girls met at Sorority they both belonged to. Their shared interest included Cindy's talent on the piano. She loved to compose the melody of songs, and Sarah wrote poems. They worked together; "just like Lennon and McCartney," the doctor sadly recounted…

That morning before Sarah walked to Cindy's house. Frank, in the bitter cold, in the wee hours of the morning, got on a chartered-bus and headed for Washington, D.C. There were twelve-buses loaded with individuals who espoused Pliartrumism. They were all headed for the Nation's capital; it was January 6, 2021. Frank, who never entered the Capital that day, stood in the cold to support Rich Pliartrum, who was still, officially, President. "His number one achievement was a tax-break for the wealthiest Americans. I remembered when I watched J6 on live-television. He never did anything good for the average guy, just for himself, his family and his billionaire buddies. And I saw the irony because it was mainly the lower-middle class on down who were his sycophants.He had every millionaire backing him. But very few of them, probably, showed up at *J6*. Millionaires never showed that day. There was one so-called billionaire. He was an actor, besides all of his other crimes, and he just played a part, in Washington D.C., for four-years. His reviews were terrible. He never conjured up *J6*. It and many other ideas, were from staffers, advisors and other politicians from the Country Club Party, and the words floated around his head until he locked in on one.

It was noon, and Pliartrum took the podium, behind thick bullet-proof glass. Frank stood amongst ten-thousand people who answered the President's call to come to the Nation's Capital city on January 6, 2021.

Mead's power was on display that day. *M-workers* twisted minds were blinded and fed a steady diet of misinformation. Glenda was the queen of *J6*, if you asked me. She outright lied to her viewers every night. A mass of hate congregated on the Ellipse that day. Frank went through security. People were packed in. Those who supported Pliartrum, were fine with America being ruled by the thugs of organized crime. The only force that could create such an historic event, and to carry it out, on this scale was *Mead*. The last time it was in Germany, under Nazi rule. The paths were open and many Germans walked upon it. It was a path to hell.

It sounded like an *F5* tornado, according to one interviewed at the scene of Pliartrum's insurrection. The flag was smeared that day, I thought. It was a catastrophe for the country. Frank and his buddies, whooped and hollered as the President spoke. Frank and his friends did not participate in what happened next. Instead, Frank was sidelined with his phone next to his ear. It felt like *Mead* worked hard that day.

———

The new song the girls collaborated on was "very nice," according to Cathy's Mom. As young Sherman played her melody on the piano, Sarah sang the lyrics that she wrote. They planned to upload it on Youtube. Doctor and Mrs. Sherman entered the den. They were ready to leave. The moment was captured by *m-watchers*. The *m-team* posted notice that m-workers would, soon, be rotated. All hands were on deck in *Mead's* world. Sarah, usually, walked back and forth between her home and Cathy's. That day, in the late afternoon, Doctor Sherman offered Sarah a ride. They were going past her home. The young teen shrugged her shoulders, and said: "okay." Cathy and Sarah sat in the back. The doctor's daughter asked her mother if Sarah could come with them. They were to attend a play at the community theater. Their nephew, the son of the doctor's brother, starred in a musical called: *Annie Get Your Gun*. The doctor received three-tickets from the young-teen, and promised that they would be there for opening night. The theater was sold-out, according to Mrs. Sherman. Cathy and Sarah planned to meet the next day.

Pat ran the vacuum cleaner in the basement because there was to be a *J6* party that night. Pat said that she never heard a thing, but the doctor claimed that after the accident every neighbor looked out their door or window. Frank's house sat on a street that had some traffic in the daytime. The street was broad enough that another bank of homes sat opposite Frank's house. It was a two-way street, but it was residential, and the speed limit was twenty-five miles per hour. When the Doctor slowed, pulled over and put his foot on the brake, *the m-workers* faced their toughest assignment. The arrangement for the death of a really good person. It always meant the *m-teams* coordinated the accident with each person's *m-team* involved. Nothing was left to chance. The coordination began days ago. Each life that Sarah touched was affected by it. Wounds to her loved ones that lasted forever. The sun had set five-minutes before, *m-worker's* data showed that all of the parties were in place. The doctor had his flashers going. Sarah, who sat behind him, took off her seatbelt, and pushed the door open. She got out only to turn and face a car with no headlights coming directly at her. She had no time to act, because it was her expiration date. She was just fourteen, and she died in her mother's arms. When Pat turned off the vacuum her neighbor was frantically coming down the basement steps. She went up two-steps at a time.

Frank returned from the *J6* that Pliartrum ordered. The president's unspeakably selfish act, placed many lives onto lanes that they never had been on before. Frank received a call from Pat when Pliartrum spoke at *J6*. The sizable number of people gathered made it impossible to hear. He received a text. "His face turned white," according to Keith.

The consequences of a child's death, especially by accident, were profound. The doctor, his wife and Cathy never arrived at the play that night. She was pronounced dead at the scene by Doctor Sherman. The Shermans stayed with Pat, who needed consoling, until Frank came in the door around midnight. The Shermans consoled the couple for hours. "We sat on the sofa and side chairs in the living room." Pat went on to tell me that Frank collapsed when we all stood to say good-bye. After the door was closed, Frank, who the doctor helped revive, sat on the sofa. His lowered head into his lap.

The funeral was very sad, I thought. I stood amongst dozens of young teens and their parents. I, finally, was placed into retirement by *Mead*. I lived on the other side of the country, and when I arrived, in my hometown, the next day. Pat told me Frank would not allow me into his house, so I stayed at a hotel. She also told me that he wanted to ban me from the funeral. My heart dropped. It was an act of evil allowed by *Mead*. People of the 21st Century who allowed people from the 20th Century to poison the stew that's eaten by people who know only goodness.

 Politics aside, goodness was never far from our hearts. Good people tolerated a lot. They don't agree. People became more tolerant of others in the last Century. Outright hatred from these little anti-boy scouts with guns was like the Nazi party in the 1930s. They got their boot into the door of the Chancellery, and it's all history from there. *Mead's* lesson was, apparently, not learned, hence, our current dilemma. What harm this disease, this scourge, this Pliartrum caused for this country, its people, its institutions, families, friendships and communities, and it's all for one simple reason: greed for money and power. Organized Crime placed their foot in the door when Pliartrum was nominated for the Country Club Party in 2016. He was only an organized crime player up to that point. Once he sat in the Oval Office, organized crime crept into the Federal system. Everything in the candy store was up for grabs. The Federal Government was like a tinker-toy when they first muscled their way into the arteries and veins, and into the fabric of this Land. Lily warned me, and she was right. She'd be amazed to learn that her comment on Youtube contributed to the exposure of Pliartrum as the simple mob-thug that he always was. "That one attribute, thug criminality, entered the Lexicon in the 1970s, we became a nation that idolized it," according to Lily. "There were gangsters, long ago, people watched, on the silver screens before television, and it wasn't a big deal; it never entered our Lexicon.

Then came the cultural side effects of the remarkable films, by Francis Ford Coppola about the mob. Everyone wanted in on it. The movies and television fed the masses great stories where the bad guys won. Pliartrum in those days admired mob bosses, and when he became of use to them he became a player. His father's wealth separated young Rich Pliartrum from the average street thug. But Pliartrum, through *Mead*, lived out his fantasy. The lane was created long ago. It's a lane for the very few. It always led to disaster for good people around the world. These teeny-weeny brains, like Pliartrum, Hitler and even back to Ivan the Terrible, always fizzled out and were destroyed. The destruction that took place led to peace and tranquility for a hundred-years. World War I and World War II taught mankind a lesson, which was learned. Evil was defeated and peace prevailed, in spite of cool relations between the US and Soviet Union. No wars were raging on European soil until Tutin supremely screwed up. Pliartrum's mouth watered when he realized that the Russian leader had bitten off more than he could chew in his invasion into a neighboring country.

A year passed, I exchanged emails with Pat, but I remained canceled in Frank's culture. Pat spent a lot of time at the Legion that year. The absence of offspring impacted their relations. They each had a separate life. Neither visited Boris on the death row.
When I heard that Frank planned a *J6* party, marking its first anniversary, on the very day that his daughter was killed, a year before, I felt his psychosis. The day was to be the unveiling of Sarah's headstone. That afternoon, I ate at a fastfood restaurant while the rest of the family was gathered in Frank's basement for a stand-up catered affair which followed the unveiling. Glenda, who did enter Frank's house, after bitching about it for decades, along with Uncle Stu both stood amongst Frank's *J6* - Bubba crew, who all brought their girlfriends. The upper echelon smiled and nodded to the lower leveled individuals. They were two different breeds of people sharing the same common interest: their support for Pliartrum. My upper-class family members were impeccably dressed. Frank got back into his jeans, as Pat and her friends prepared for the party. The dress-code called for jeans and t-shirts; Pliartrum t-shirts, of course. Frank had more than a dozen in a box in the basement's utility room.

Fifty people gathered that night. Frank went all out. Tiki-torches, ablaze, were placed ten-feet apart around the perimeter of the chain link fence. The heated swimming pool and the lights of the watering hole were turned on. A handful of men and women were in the water, as they gossiped and consumed alcohol from its containers.

I didn't go to the catered lunch because I wasn't invited. I waited until the next day, one-minute after midnight, to go to his *J6 - one year anniversary party*. There was a time when I, without doubt, should've never come to a social gathering. Especially a Pliartrum one. My seethed nerves prickled when I consumed any of their poison, even for a second. But, something happened. It happened before. I was used to it by now. *Mead* choreographed a marvelous dance for myself and the Pliartrum faithful. The *m-team* and *Mead* served me too many times for me to count. Just like the costa nostra, *Mead* had a service for me to perform. You might say that I was in rehearsals for sixty-years, and now, *Mead* revealed my purpose to me. It was hard to imagine that after all of these decades, my help from *Mead* was to be repaid in the 21st Century, and after all that time, it came to me, Frank and his friends. None of the regular neighbors that I knew from when I "traveled," were present. These people were brought to face myself. I, in turn, was brought to face *Mead*. *It* enforced the *Executives' big view*. Summoned, *Mead* carried out orders. Directives that changed societies, forever.

When I walked through the gate, it took just seconds to hear Frank yell: "What are you doing? Why are you here? Keith spoke up and said:
"He's brainwashed by the People Party." I heard laughter. Chance piped up and yelled: "Yeah, we want to kill the People Party. Pliartrum has all of you ready for the ovens." Guests hooped and hollered. Frank remained silent. The music from the outdoor speakers stopped and so did

everybody else. I thought that I, once again, stood in front of a classroom of elementary school children. Kids were frozen by their *m-workers* to open up all channels to receive important *Mead* content.

They looked like a mean bunch, but I've taken over classrooms in my days, which were deemed uncontrollable according to the teacher's note to the substitute."Call for the principal if the student, whose desk was up against the chalkboard, acts out." The fourth grader was a scattered mess. Her hair was cut as if she had done it. She took her seat. The rest of the class did the same. I told them what I've told to children ever since my make-over. No longer was I hated. I was welcomed and respected, and it was all due to *Mead's* words. Like I said, before, I never took credit for someone else's work. However, they even impacted the student who had all of the problems. She, and the rest of the class, presented no problems that day. My note to the teacher was that the students did well today. The kicker, however, was three-weeks later, when I was at the same school again. I supervised the kids who were on the playground. As I stood there the fourth-grade girl, who had all of the problems, ran up to me and said: "I wanted to thank you, Mister Isaac, you taught me how to be good." As she walked away I realized that the words in the shower that day were magical.

They were simple words that carried a lot of weight. With my name on the board, and all of the students seated, I began: I said that: "Everybody has a good side to them and a bad side, and when you come to school you need to show your good side. You need to show it to your teacher. You need to show it to your fellow classmates, and you need to show it to yourself. Because you need to be aware that it's there, because your good side is a very important part of you, and you need to bring it out and use it!" I went on with their attention: "When we're at home our brothers and sisters like to show us their bad sides, and we turn right around, and show them ours. It's an automatic reflex," I explained and demonstrated, "just like when the doctor hits your knee with a little rubber hammer your leg will always pop up." I continued: "What do you think that your Mom and Dad would do if they went to work, and they were silly and goofy, or they were mean or mad. What do you think would happen to them if they did that? The answer always came back: "They'd be fired." I'd agree with them and added. So, school is a very important place. And when we are in public, which means that you're not at home, and this is your job, and you'll have this job for many years, and then you'll have a grown-up job just like your parents. So when you come to school, show it: Because when we show our good side, good things happen to us. When we show our bad side, bad things happen. So when you find yourself in an important place, it's important to show you at your best. Never at your worst."

As the steam rose from the heated water all eyes were on me, and they were red with fire in them. But, I felt warmth in mine and I knew why: *Mead*. I never saw people's expressions so stark. The power of hate was in their eyes. Not the power of goodness. I hadn't seen that since I was a boy and I saw black and white photos of World War II. They were Germans and they were swallowed up by the Nazis, who carried the power of hate. They spread it throughout the land. Nobody was immune to it. Either be a good Nazi or else.

Mead revealed knowledge, to me, just bits at a time. I witnessed how *its* words impacted unruly young kids in a classroom, but I wasn't so sure I could grab and keep their attention.of those that surrounded me. Alcohol was the main fuel that generated them, as each held a bottle of beer in their hand. In one swoop, those gathered were taken aback. I looked at Frank and he was stunned. Pat too. They were all stunned. Just like in school. Just like in my last MH job when I presented words that came to me, and that I wrote down.

The pool was ringed by Pliartrum's people. They looked at me with contempt. I, for that moment, felt that I held their attention. These were, exactly, the kinds of people who I needed to reach. Good people who've latched on to evil, Pliartrum. It's not their fault. It's happened many times before in history, it's a powerful spell that they were under. I tried to reach Frank, he stopped talking to me. We haven't spoken for five-years now. And, it's all because of one man. I had a message for him and the others gathered. As my eyes moved around the perimeter of the pool, Uncle Stu and Glenda came out of the house. They held mixed drinks. They were dressed up like it was a swanky affair. With jaws dropped they stared, and it seemed as if they moved in slow-motion as they joined the others around the chlorinated watering hole. As the steam wiggled out of the H2O, they just continued staring at me like I was a bug in a mason jar. The *m-workers* were ordered into full conflict mode. They played both sides. However, *m-watchers* very rarely interfered in these types of human interaction. The amount of data that was generated by these types of incidents determined that it was a life changing event. Each player's *m-teams* connected. *Mead's* motive was the same it's been since the first brother against brother occurred. Cain slew Abel, and it's never stopped since.

I never thought, for one second, that my school pitch to kids would be effective on followers of Pliartrum, so I began by saying: "We are all being tested. We are tested as children and as teenagers. We are tested as individuals when we move forward with our lives as adults. We're tested each moment of each day.

One guest spoke up: "Who gives a fuck what you say."

Everybody remained silent. I never hesitated. "*Mead* is what it's called. We're puppets on *its* strings. *It's* testing us. *It* provided pathways to carry out our wishes we hold close to the heart. Our society. Us as individuals, from birth to death, are tested. Every interaction we have with ourselves and others produces data, it's given to *Mead*. *It* gives it to the Executives, Jesus, Mohammed and Buddah, who presents it to God, it's that crucial.

"Go to Hell," I heard.

"It's to gauge our morality." We are slowly evaporating. We're going backwards instead of forward in time. And all that mankind gained over the fifty-sixty years, in civil rights, women's rights, all kinds of rights for the protection of people and animals alike. People learned that they had the right to live freely without harassment. To be cordial and civil when we're in public. Mead, probably, understands when we act out at home behind closed doors. If you hate people, you're wrong. Do you actually, for one second, think that *God*, or your *Executive* wants you to hate your fellowman? Hitler wanted Germans to do that, and they did it. Now there's Pliartrum and he asks for the same exact things that Hitler wanted and tried to get away with, but he didn't and neither will Pliartrump. Tragedy breeds tragedy. *J6* demonstrated to me that Pliartrum and Tutin must be fought, just like Hitler and Mussolini in WWII. I am prepared to carry on Lily's work. When I served in the military a long war had just ended. I used to think, mistakenly, that my service to the country went awry, because I never appreciated the democracy that I lived in and served as a seaman. Those were carefree days in the military. Somehow, history never mattered in the latter half of the 1970s. But, Pliartrum changed how I felt. He posted a response to Lily's comment, and now, she was no longer alive to fight for it. I took her place in my mind. And I was determined to fight Pliartrum. I sensed a shift in the gathered group, a few guys met off to the side. I finished with the thought: Do you want an America where the thugs are in charge? Well, I don't!" Frank and his crew who stood behind me pulled me away from where I stood. They put me on the ground. Each took one of my limbs. They swung me back and forth before they hurled me into the water. Everybody laughed and clapped their hands.

Chapter 30

Lily wanted to change every heart in America. Uncle Stu wanted his Country Club Party in power with Pliartrum at its helm. Pliartrum fancied himself the most powerful man in history. Pliartrum, Jr. saw himself as his father's successor. Glenda fit right in with all of the grift and the greed. Boris hoped for a reprieve. Frank was more radical than ever, as his social media indicated. Pat, for all practical purposes, was sidelined from alcoholism and her Pliartrum narcotic. Manuel was a different story. His crime horrified me, as did Boris'. They were like two tropical storms in the Gulf of Mexico. They met, and they increased in strength by the hour. It became a frenzied category-five hurricane that they conspired with evil. Each carried it out, and imagined themselves doing, not just once, but often, everyday; they craved it. They planned and acted, both in a murderous rage. Manuel's *m-team* ordered the *m-watchers*, and, subsequently, the *m-workers* that there was another emergency case.

  The *Mead Guide* was very clear. Chiseled into stone were *laws* which governed every case of matricide, patricide or parricide. Collected, deep-data instantaneously moved up the chain. *Mead*, in consultation with an *Executive*, made the final call. *Mead* waited for an answer. Whether in the midst of horror, just before the act and the soul stopped and turned around. Or that he continued and crept forward with murder in his eyes. Every breath from the potential killer generated deep data. It added up all of the fantasies. Multiplied by what *Mead* and the *m-team's* data showed.

They merged, and it went straight to heart. The killing was set and he was ready to go. With his act, two lives were cracked open, one literally. It fed darkness to diabolical evil. *Mead*, issued approval to proceed based on two factors. One was Lily's history of sacrifice and goodness. The other was what young Manuel planned to do. They were placed on their road to oblivion. One returned to whence it came. The other was stored in a cell. He was isolated from Society. *Mead* imposed life. It was meant as a living hell. Manuel became a desperado. He aimed for safety through power; it was futile, however. He was targeted whenever he was in the general population. He attempted suicide in his first year; *Mead* would have none of it. Soon he fought like a gladiator with a crude weapon he designed out of a piece of plastic. It landed him in solitary confinement. After he came out; he had fire in his eyes. Eventually, however, he was permitted by his *m-workers* to join an Hispanic gang for his protection. When he first arrived he wasn't accepted. Manuel worried. It happened much later, but, eventually, *Mead* ordered action from the *m-team*. All of Manuel's *m-team* was on alert. In the end, the minor received protection, he said in an email to Pat. But, words meant little to *Mead*, people said a lot of things. Most of it was classified as gibberish. He wanted Lily out of his life. He, in the sickest throes of his mental illness, actually, thought that he could get away with it.

As for me, the lessons that I learned, I paid, dearly, for. I never understood my behavior, but I sorely wanted to. I understood my sexuality. Was it wrong? Yes, for me. Not for anyone else. It was wrong just for me. It was the path I ignored for fifty-years. I never felt love because *Mead* ordered that I wasn't supposed to. Ergo, the message that I received, on the balcony, at the Temple, was not a request. I wouldn't do it voluntarily; so it was imposed upon me. I never knew how I transformed into a mindless, although nonviolent, criminal as a youth. I never changed. I couldn't. I committed crimes against other people's intangible assets. It never belonged to me, but.I took it, again and again. I gave my employer's property away to others; some I knew, and others I didn't. Hundreds and hundreds of dollars of an employer's goods went unpaid for over the months. I never thought about it, therefore, I never understood it or other things like why I had no friends. I tried being a part of society, but I never fit in.

Mead saw to it, however. I was given an important gift. I helped others whose minds needed care and attention like my own. I wasn't perfect at it, I made my share of mistakes. But, it all came from the heart. And I learned. Eventually, everything changed for me, but it was only after I received my bipolar diagnosis from the VA. I thanked *Mead*. I desperately sought answers that were, ultimately, revealed.to me.

 It took time. In the end, Mead gave and taught everybody something. Boris was supported, publicly, by celebrities and spiritually, by Rabbis. He learned the ways of God. Lily expired from the rage of a sociopath. She, most likely, learned that her kindness backfired. Pat got more heartache on top of her alcoholism and her addiction to Pliartrum's drugs. She learned, the hard way, that people who coped better, with life, fared better. On the other hand, Glenda received good-evil from *Mead*; she was protected and encouraged. Uncle Stu learned that he and other Country Club Party members were free people, when they were really Hitlerized. The same power, *Mead*, that placed the German people, at that time, under political hypnosis, did it again. This time, however, it was the United States of America who *Mead* targeted. Finally, there was Pliartrum. He should've learned not to respond to an average citizen's comment on Youtube. His awkward son got the message too. He learned as much as Glenda, zero. Because there was no goodness in the Pliartrum family. His kids were greedy leeches; and just like their father no one stood on his own.

As for my heart, for the first time in my life, I tapped into my personal goodness not my professional, which came from the heart. I never knew what turned it on and off. When I walked through the door of the Meyer's Club, it had changed my life. *Mead* arranged it. I walked on a very special path, but I lost it, eventually, at each of my MH jobs. Later, I understood that it was all planned. I did well for a while after that my own MH worsened, and along with cluster headaches I became a wreck, and I remained so for years before I bounced back; it happened four times in thirty-years.

Lily was different, she never lost her mind. As she grew up she never crossed anyone. Yet, she became a sacrificial lamb. Manuel's machismo was triggered by events, after which, he craved her death. In his eyes she had wronged him one time too many. Her overprotective parenting lit a powder keg. It was toxic to him, and it was concocted by a mind that accepted and responded to internal-stimuli. He saw himself in motion. He relished the thoughts. The young mind performed his deadly deed. I understood, later, that *M-planners, m-developers and m-coordinators*, in cooperation with *m-watchers* and *m-workers* were in sync with Lily's *m-team*, who, by decree, relinquished Lily's soul, which was covered under the *Mead Guidelines,* a policy and procedure manual for all *m-team* personnel. *M-workers* positions required recertification. It followed their last assignment. Lily's *m-workers* were carefully debriefed when they returned. They learned in training that they had the power to change a person's destiny, like Manuel or Boris, that is, if it fell within *Mead's* rules, which were issued from above.. Whatever held each back until the pivotal moment, only *Mead,* the *Executives* and *God* knew. It was the intent that posted red flags to *m-watchers*, who knew that the person acted out what they fantasized and desired. *Mead* provided the real-estate, and the *M-workers* built the path. *Mead* led the individual astray. It was tolerated. Tolerance was a very important human quality, which was impossible for some people to show. It could never be called upon. It came from the heart. There were people who weren't interested in personal growth. They never improved their lot in Mead's assessment of the data. Or, they and their leaders ignored truth and tolerance. Thus, they remained steadfast and ignorant. I was one of them when I was younger. I was jammed between two slices of moldy bread, Mom and Dad, who never wanted me. I should've understood, long ago, that I courted immorality, and consciously felt free of guilt because there was something wrong with me. It went on for decades. I, nor anyone else, stopped me. I was free to roam wild, and I continued. I made a complete idiot of myself in the process. It took me back to a moment that I vividly remembered. I was a boy again, and I rode in the car, the one headed for the mall. How, from that moment on, I accepted and believed what I heard on that day, and how it impacted me for the rest of my life.

Mistakenly, I learned that cuteness was important. I walked a long way before I realized that I was wrong and that I was lost. My aunt told me that I looked like an angel, ergo I thought that I was cute. I went through my early years with that in mind. It followed me into my teens. Much later, as an adult, I realized that I was completely wrong. However, one day, in particular, when I was the substitute teacher, it only proved that I still had a lot to learn. I was assigned to a third-grade class. Some kids were busy with their pencils and worked at their desks. Others were with me in a reading group. We sat on small chairs in a circle. Before we got started one of the kids spoke up and caught everyone's attention. He pointed to the boy next to him and he said to me: "He said you're ugly." It was softball. I should've hit it out of the park. Instantaneously, any normal adult would respond with the obvious answer. Especially, when it came off the cuff from a youngster who should have received a totally different response than the one that I gave to him. This was the moment for all of them. I failed. I never responded with the correct answer. My presence, unfortunately, delivered the wrong message. The simple truth of the old adage that; "*beauty comes from within; it doesn't matter what someone looks like on the outside; it's what's on the inside that counts.*" Instead, I sat there like a fool and replied: "Well, he's entitled to his opinion." I not only missed the softball, I struck out. I, instantly, should've spouted out the right answer. Much later, I felt ashamed that I didn't, honestly.

My mental health education taught me that people who weren't physically beautiful were often beautiful inside. And some people who were candy to the eyes, were very ugly inside. I was one of them, I concluded. That's how I knew. I crossed many people's paths. My innate goodness surfaced. I worked on it a lot, and I taught it, along with the lesson plan for that day. I was always amazed by it. Simple words that came together; it made such a difference; it always set the right tone.

Those words that came to me in the shower connected with children. They each used their goodness, some for the very first time. They brought it out and used it. They showed it to me. They showed it to their fellow classmates. And, they showed it to themselves.

Glenda was a perfect example. She was a popular socialite, but I knew that she was ugly inside. Something else that was ugly was Pliartrum. He didn't just bad mouth someone who he thought wronged him, he was out for blood. He ordered his Muscle to intimidate his followers and opponents, even the average citizen. They were experienced thugs. But, regular American people saw through him. After all, I told

Lily: "I saw *The Godfather* fifty-times." Apparently, Plairtum believed that nobody knew his dirty little secret. The takeover of America by Organized Crime. *Don Corleone*, if reported correctly, turned over in his grave at the news. The mob always wanted to buy judges and politicians, to put them in their little pockets. Now they demanded judgeships and political office themselves. Their thievery had no boundaries. Glenda and Uncle Stu saw people like me and Lily as dead meat. On television, one night, a follower at a Pliartrum rally, in a silent second, spoke up and bellowed: "When do I get to use my AR-15 on those bastards?" Pliartrum's crowd hooted, hollered and applauded, enthusiastically, their agreement.

Bubba did that a lot. He hooted and hollered when it was *J6*. He hooted and hollered Pliartrum's attacks on our institutions, primarily, the Justice Department, the FBI, ATF and other institutions dedicated to catching criminals, like the IRS. These were the same institutions that organized crime feared and who the Federal government fought, everyday, to weed out and place into jail. What happened, the mob never thought possible, even in their wildest dreams. The leader of organized crime in America became Pliartrum All he knew was that he was always right about everything and that he wanted to rip-off the Feds as much as he could. He was never challenged by anyone in the Country Club Party. Why would they? He did nothing wrong. He took no responsibility for any of his presidential crimes, yet alone the others before and after he was president. The guy was a petty-crook. He was a b-list celebrity from a washed up television series. He was defeated, eventually. Glenda learned the hard way too. She got cocky on-air, one night. The PROX NEWS' owner read her emails and texts. They were quite provocative and were reported on. When made public, she lost every sponsor. She was canceled with a ten-minute notice. She lost a lot. Her home outside of New York City, sold. Her penthouse in NYC, sold. Her perks were all canceled too.

Mead played real hard, at times, with the folks in the Country Club Party. After all, they were on the wrong side of every major issue. It was *Mead* who put them there. Why not? They alienated, demonized, and fought everything that was decent, fair and tolerant. Again, it was *Mead* who kept track of their cockeyed ideas and conspiracy theories and theorists. So, *Mead* created the conflict and blinded Pliartrum's people from a mountain of truth. If they only knew that they were being played the whole time. Bubba was the sucker. Evil flourished. The Country Club Party elite participated or stood by and watched it as it all happened. That's because Pliartrum, *"made them an offer that they couldn't refuse.*

That day, I looked at the graveyard digger. Nearby, a man in a dark blue suit and ray-ban sunglasses acted. I looked around, ~~Sarah~~ Pat was gone, ~~and so was Pat~~. Frank and Uncle Stu stood shoulder to shoulder. Frank stood erect and took in a deep breath. He watched the stranger. That's all that I knew. Much later, I learned from a seasoned *m-worker*, who trained me to become an *m-worker*, and who was now an *m-watcher*, was at his funeral that day. Thus, he could share what happened to me. The *m-worker* pulled out his *m-cellphone*, and I read the account. It made the front page of the *New York Times* website. The story gave the graveyard digger's account. A man produced a semi-automatic weapon, with a silencer. He took aim at me and emptied his clip. The goon approached my lifeless body, kicked me in the face and said: "That's from President Pliartrum."

The End

;

Made in the USA
Columbia, SC
17 November 2024

46443920R00117